the COMIC STRIP

Big Fat Book of Knowledge

Sally Kindberg
and Tracey Turner

BLOOMSBURY
LONDON BERLIN NEW YORK SYDNEY

For Tom, Toby and Wellington – T.T.

To my robotic friends – S.K.

Bloomsbury Publishing, London, Berlin, New York and Sydney

This omnibus edition first published in Great Britain in September 2011
by Bloomsbury Publishing Plc
49–51 Bedford Square, London, W1CB 3DP

The Comic Strip History of the World first published
by Bloomsbury Publishing Plc in 2008

The Comic Strip History of Space first published
by Bloomsbury Publishing Plc in 2009

The Comic Strip Greatest Greek Myths first published
by Bloomsbury Publishing Plc in 2010

A CIP catalogue record for this book is available from the British Library

ISBN 978 1 4088 0824 5

FSC
www.fsc.org
MIX
Paper from
responsible sources
FSC® C019704

Printed in Singapore by Tien Wah Press Pte Ltd

1 3 5 7 9 10 8 6 4 2

www.bloomsbury.com

Featuring

History
of the
World

History
of
Space

Greatest
Greek Myths

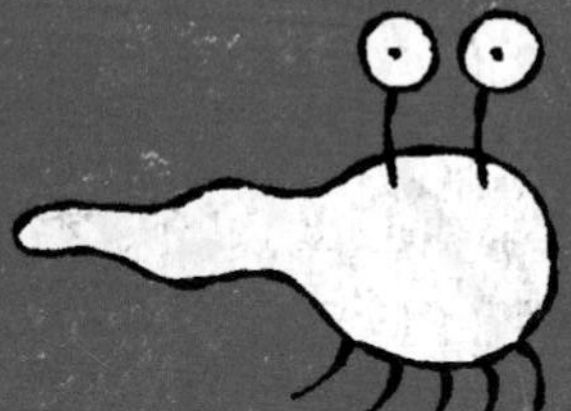

the COMIC STRIP History of the World

Contents

How it all started (probably) 1
Early man 2
Civilisation is born! 4
Ancient Egypt 6
Ancient China 10
The Indus Valley 12
Minoans 14
Ancient Greece 16
Alexander the Great. 20
The Rise of the Roman Empire 22
The Fall of the Roman Empire 24
Barbarians! 26
Attila the Hun 28
The Polynesians 30
The Dark Ages. 32
Vikings! 36
Mongols 38
The Moors in Spain 40
African Empires. 41
War! (lots of it) 42

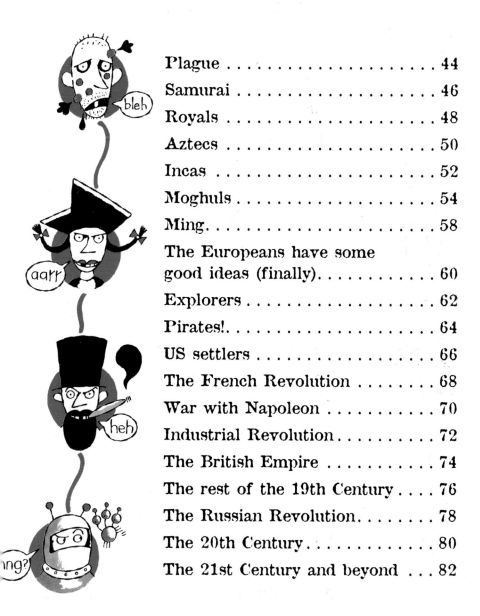

Plague 44
Samurai 46
Royals 48
Aztecs 50
Incas 52
Moghuls 54
Ming. 58
The Europeans have some
good ideas (finally). 60
Explorers 62
Pirates!. 64
US settlers 66
The French Revolution 68
War with Napoleon 70
Industrial Revolution 72
The British Empire 74
The rest of the 19th Century 76
The Russian Revolution. 78
The 20th Century. 80
The 21st Century and beyond . . . 82

HOW IT ALL STARTED (PROBABLY)
Several billion years ago in space there was a whopping
BIG BANG!!!
I'm out of here!
WHOOSH
distant galaxies
WHOOSH
LATER...
stinky gases
ZAP
ZAP
ZAP
the EARTH was formed.
First there was a sort of simple cell soup...
blip
blop
then things got more complicated.
250 million years ago
I fancy a walk!
LAND
Later still...
nrgh!
65 million years ago there was a sudden CATASTROPHE.
extinct
Then MAMMALS took over.
hi there

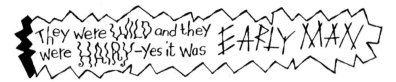

They were WILD and they were HAIRY – Yes it was EARLY MAN

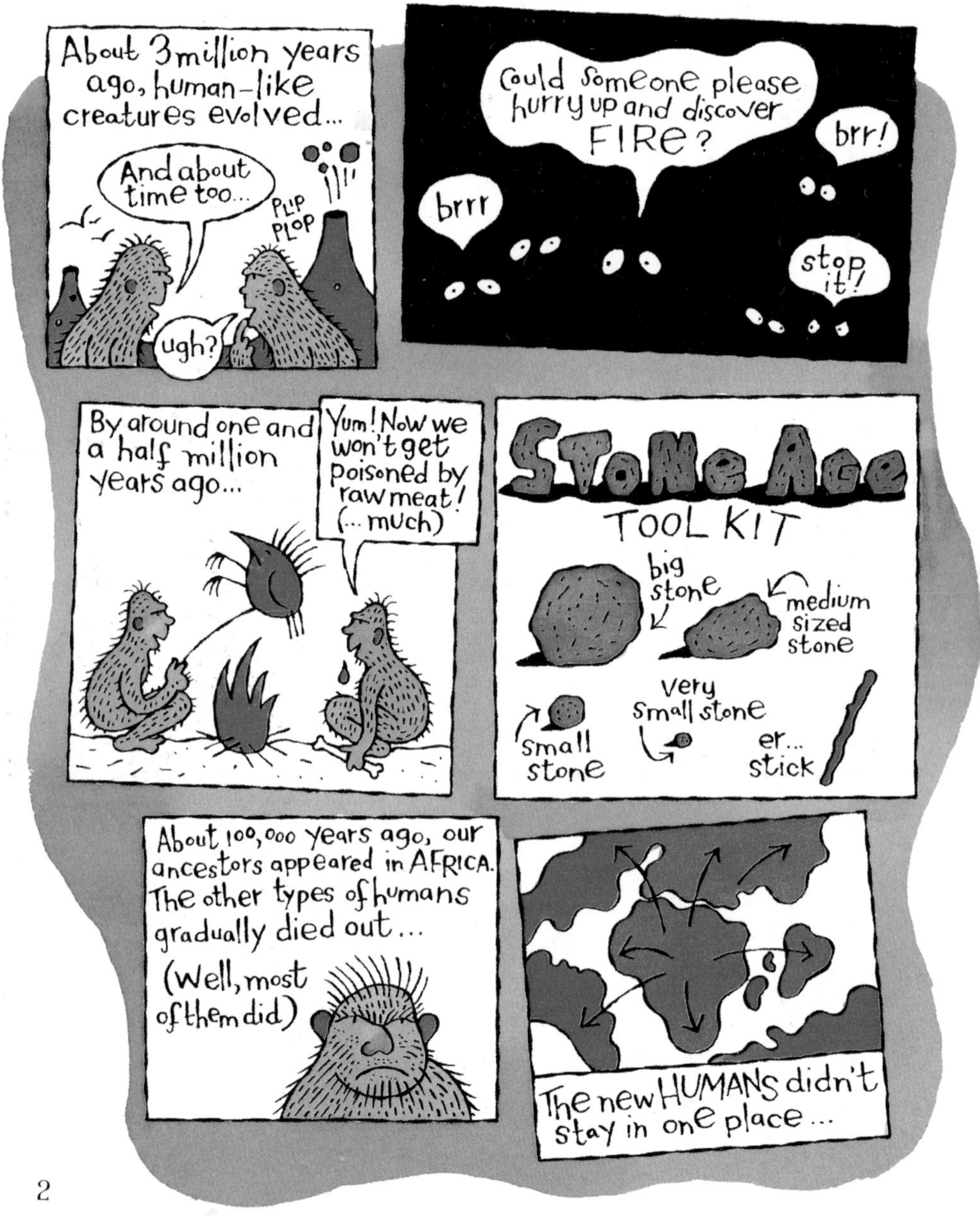
About 3 million years ago, human-like creatures evolved...
And about time too...
PLIP PLOP
ugh?
Could someone please hurry up and discover FIRE?
brrr
brr!
stop it!
By around one and a half million years ago...
Yum! Now we won't get poisoned by raw meat! (...much)
STONE AGE TOOL KIT
big stone
medium sized stone
small stone
very small stone
er... stick
About 100,000 years ago, our ancestors appeared in AFRICA. The other types of humans gradually died out...
(Well, most of them did)
The new HUMANS didn't stay in one place...

People spent their time hunting...
HAAAARGH!
Uh?
HAAAARGH!
gathering...
Lunch!
Lunch!
and generally roaming about...
(Oh ... and along the way someone, somewhere, invented this)
Newfangled nonsense!
mutter mutter
until...
Whew!
I could do with a nice rest
I know... let's settle down here!
Ooh! You talking commit-ment?

and so...

CIVILISATION IS BORN!

TOWNs grew where people settled
bleat
bleat

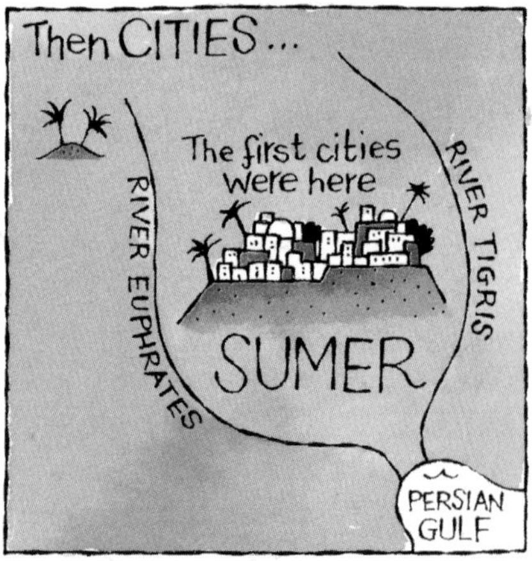
Then CITIES...
The first cities were here
RIVER EUPHRATES
RIVER TIGRIS
SUMER
PERSIAN GULF

Then a whole EMPIRE...

BLACK SEA
CASPIAN SEA
MEDITERRANEAN SEA
AKKADIAN EMPIRE
RIVER TIGRIS
RIVER EUPHRATES
PERSIAN GULF
I'm Sargon
This is the first ever empire
and it's mine, all mine!
har har har
fancy emperor's beard

Until ...
urk
Sargon died...
The empire expanded...
VERY LARGE AKKADIAN EMPIRE
and declined...
and disappeared.
Different empires came and went in Mesopotamia
RIVER TIGRIS
RIVER EUPHRATES
including...
BABYLON
it's THE destination
ancient travel agent
We've got a Babylonian special this weekend!
Not one of the 7 Wonders, is it?
Too right! Hanging Gardens, half price.
In the end Mesopotamia became part of the huge Persian empire.
It's ours, all ours!
har har har etc.
ouch

Meanwhile, other civilisations were now popping up all over the place...

Ancient Egypt
EGYPT a long time ago...
Oooh a river!
Nice here, isn't it?
Then...
Oi!
I'm king Narmer
Unite or else!
I say!
Later... the first pyramids were built
NEW!
Later still... more pyramids and a bit of conquering.
I hear they've got a great view of the afterlife.
I like a nice Egyptian!
NILE

Even later still ... tombs were built for the Valley of the Kings.
Pyramids are just so last year!
MEDITERRANEAN SEA
LOWER EGYPT
RIVER NILE
RED SEA
UPPER EGYPT
EGYPT was divided in two, then reunited, then divided again as ...
the Nubians ...
BIFF
then the Assyrians ...
BIFF
then the Persians all ruled EGYPT for a while.
BIFF
EGYPT was conquered more thoroughly in 332 BC ...
BIFF BIFF
Not again!!
MORE NILE

The ancient Egyptians had lots of strange gods...

Er... more milk?
peck peck
hnng!
urrg!
I'm sure he's very sweet deep down.
Just make yourself at home.
Really... anything for attention!

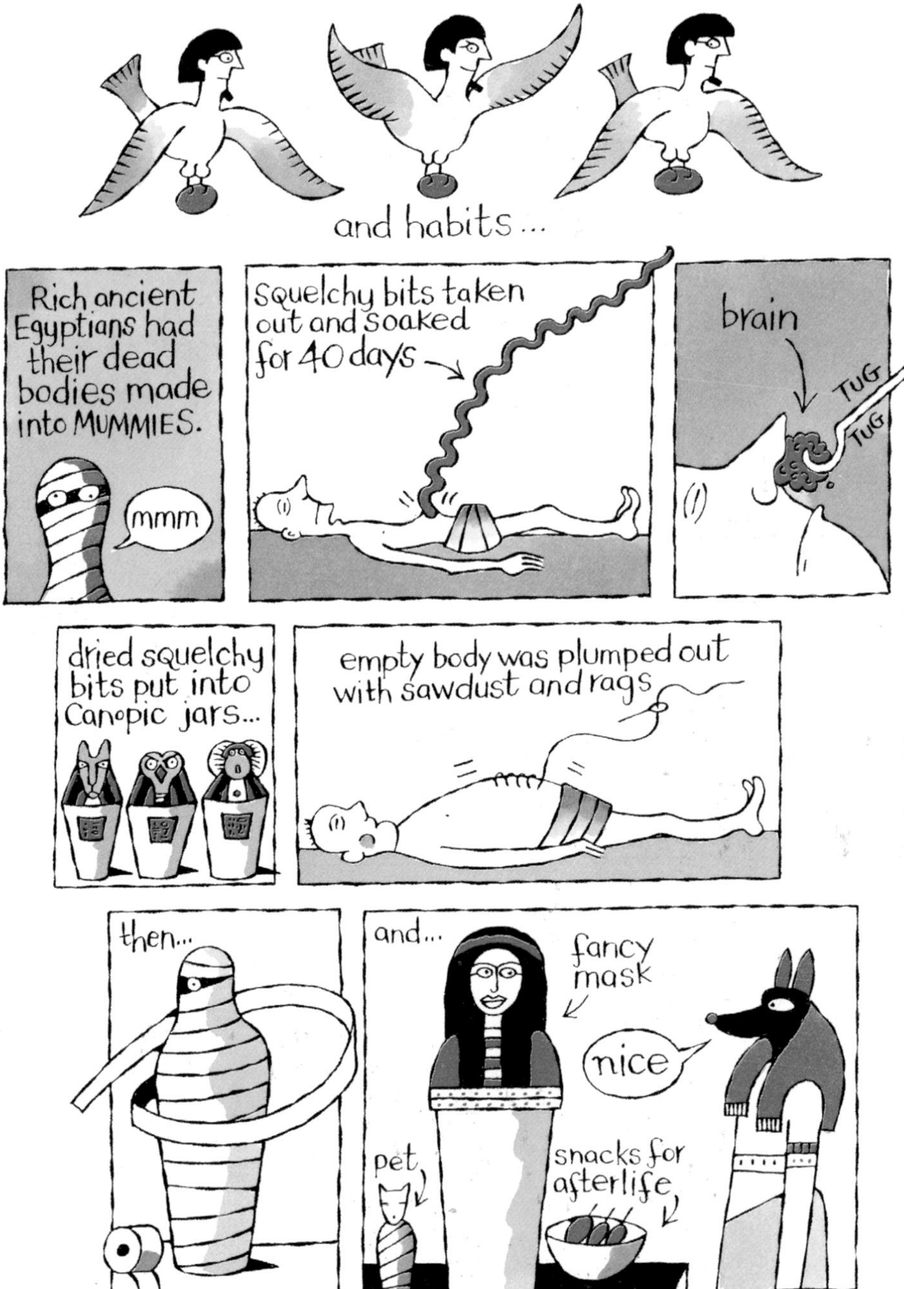

and habits ...
Rich ancient Egyptians had their dead bodies made into MUMMIES.
mmm
squelchy bits taken out and soaked for 40 days
brain
TUG
TUG
dried squelchy bits put into Canopic jars...
empty body was plumped out with sawdust and rags
then...
and...
fancy mask
nice
pet
snacks for afterlife

Meanwhile, over in ...

ANCIENT CHINA

People settled in the Huang He (Yellow River) valley...
It's so handy for the shops
and a nice view

They were ruled by DYNASTIES (powerful families)
I'm a Zhou
I'm one of the Xias
I'm one of the Shangs

Then came a period known as the WARRING STATES (for obvious reasons)...

until QIN SHI HUANGDI defeated the other kings, united CHINA, and ...
I'm the First Emperor
and don't you forget it!
har har
ghh!

Build me a Great Big Wall!
Now!
That'll Keep out the Northerners!
Qin's Great Wall
MONGOLIA
BEIJING
CHINA
Qin Shi Huangdi had a life-size army made out of clay to fight for him in the afterlife.
QUICK march!
In their spare time the Chinese invented porcelain ... and gunpowder. WHOOPS!
Soon after Qin died came the HAN dynasty.
urk
There were more dynasties after that...
SUI
TANG
SONG
YUAN
MING
QING
PAPER was a Chinese invention too

And further south...

the Indus Valley

civilisation had existed for hundreds of years. But we don't know much about it due to the...

MISTS of TIME

Lothal
Harappa
Mohenjo-Daro
RIVER INDUS
mysterious civilisation
Arabian Sea
INDIA
This has been a puzzle for archaeologists
But we've not found any big temples or palaces
Mohenjo-Daro was the biggest city in the area
Maybe they built them out of wood?
Or maybe they didn't have any?
Hmm
Maybe we'll never know
SIGH

They had a written language...
scritch scratch
cough cough
but we can't understand it!
Bother!
But we do know that they had really good drains, toilets and sewers...
more MISTS of TIME
This area gave birth to... the world's first dentists! At least, as far as we know
heh heh
Trust me, I'm an ancient dentist!
ancient filling
ancient molar
No one knows why they disappeared. Unlike another ancient civilisation...

MINOANS

...the island of CRETE, 2000 BC...

The MINOAN civilisation's biggest city was Knossos, with a huge royal palace five storeys high...
All mod. cons and amazing wall paintings!
luxury flats!
Paved roads!

Look after my snake, will you?
snake cult priestess
ssss
All right. Then I'm off for a bit of leaping.
I want to use my new FLUSHING loo!

The Minoans were a bit strange in some ways...
TONITE ONLY!! BVLL LEAPING
Ooh this is fun!
Snort

But they were also very clever...
Let's make this fiendishly complicated!
Tee hee

MINOAN writing, known as LINEAR A, has still not been deciphered...
Bother!

Round about 1550 BC, the nearby SANTORINI volcano erupted...
WHOOSH!
urk
urk
urk
Crete

Shortly followed by...

Bash
ooof
ooh
thump

Until ... the MYCENAEAN GREEKS nobbled the Minoans and became top dogs in Greece for the next few hundred years ... then...

ANCIENT GREECE

Invaders from the North arrived

DELPHI
THEBES
ATHENS
SICYON
CORINTH
MYCENAE
ARGOS
OLYMPIA
SPARTA
They built separate city-states all over Greece
Those Spartans are a funny lot!
Never trust an Athenian, I say.
Have you seen the state of those Olympian beards?
The biggest city-state was ATHENS. Some states were ruled by kings but ATHENS was a DEMOCRACY.
And we shall all be equal and vote in political elections!
Hurrah!
Yes, hurrah!
Hurrah
Er, not you women actually
That's a bit unfair, isn't it?
Tut!
Boo!
What!!
...and not slaves, obviously.

As I was saying, everyone is equal
... apart from women, slaves and foreigners.
Tut!
Shame!
Hurrah!
Boo!
That rules most of us out then!

But while Greece was divided... the huge PERSIAN empire attacked

Nnngh!
Stamp
Aaaargh! We've had it!
What if all the states fight them together?
Those Persians look scary!
Gnash
Grrr
Brilliant idea!

The war with the Persians went on for decades. Until finally...

...the united Greeks won

Cough cough
Whew
About time too

This left time for other things, such as THINKING

Hmm...
What is everything made of?
What is justice?
Does anything exist independently???
Got it!
c
b
a
!
I could murde
a cup of tea

... and DRAMA

(Some of it was—ahem—rather rude!)

... RELIGION

... ART and ARCHITECTURE
New this year! IONIC columns

But peace between states didn't last long. ATHENS and SPARTA went to war...

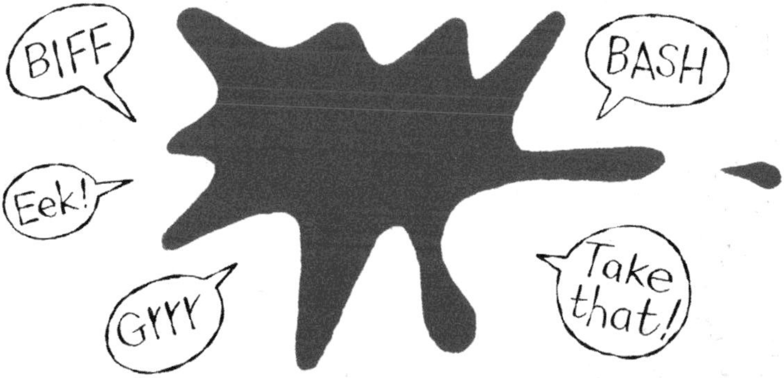
BIFF
BASH
Eek!
GRRR
Take that!

The rest of Greece got involved too
They're having a massive punch-up in the Peloponnese!
Let's get down there!

After nearly 30 years of war, Sparta won
Oh, I give up!

It wasn't long before another army arrived in Greece...

ALEXANDER the GREAT

ALEXANDER the GREAT, king of Macedonia, was on the rampage...
Hi, I'm Alex...
and I'm GREAT
snort
snort
whinny
He conquered GREECE...
urk
urk
BASH
BIFF
the old PERSIAN empire... there was a lot of it...
WHACK
So it needed conquering twice...
WALLOP
Oh no again
Some of EGYPT (where he was made a god)
Thanks
ooh
And some of INDIA...

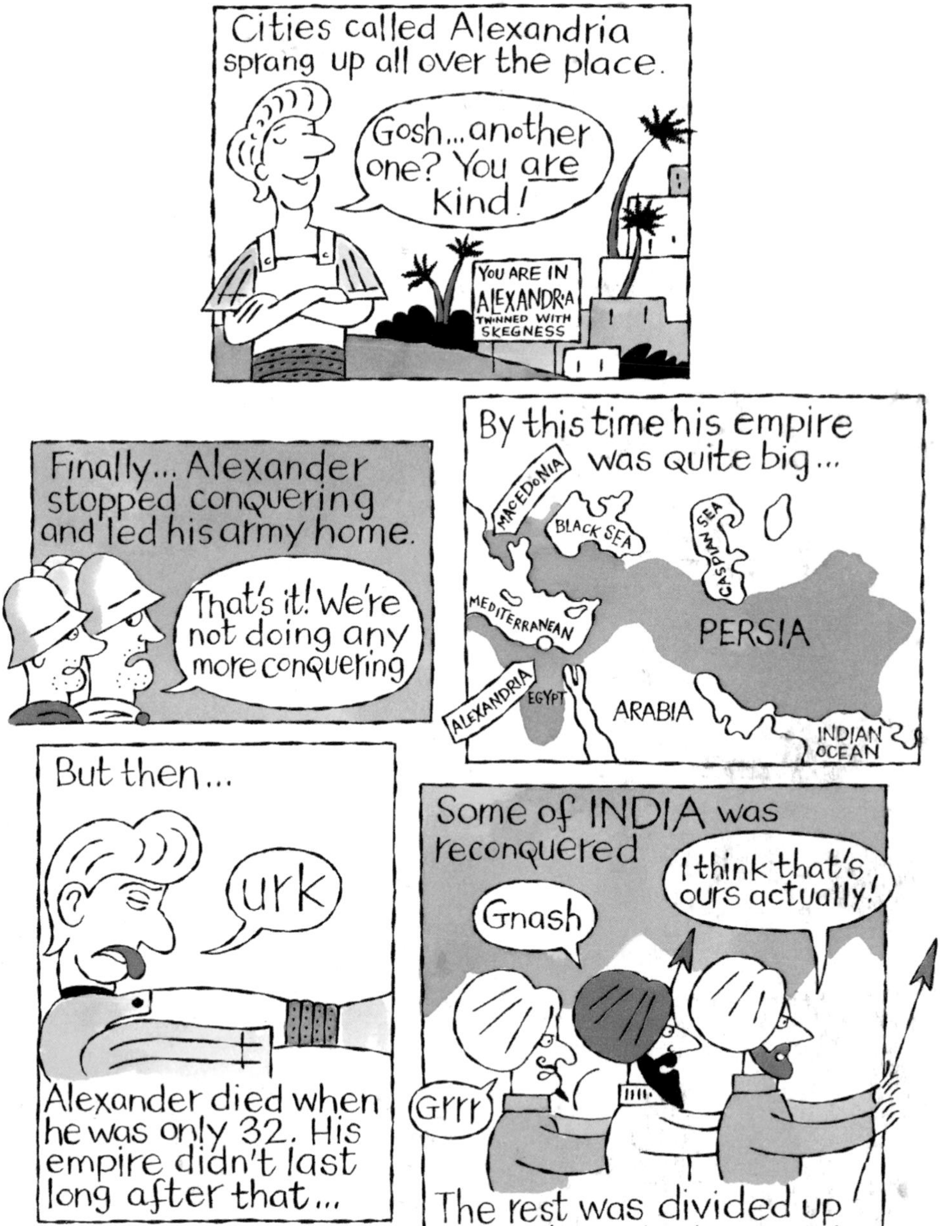
Cities called Alexandria sprang up all over the place.
Gosh...another one? You are kind!
YOU ARE IN ALEXANDRIA TWINNED WITH SKEGNESS
Finally... Alexander stopped conquering and led his army home.
That's it! We're not doing any more conquering
By this time his empire was quite big...
MACEDONIA
BLACK SEA
CASPIAN SEA
MEDITERRANEAN
PERSIA
ALEXANDRIA
EGYPT
ARABIA
INDIAN OCEAN
But then...
urk
Alexander died when he was only 32. His empire didn't last long after that...
Some of INDIA was reconquered
Gnash
I think that's ours actually!
Grrr
The rest was divided up among Alexander's generals.

Meanwhile, another lot of conquering was going on...

THE RISE OF THE ROMAN EMPIRE

Hello, we're the ancient Romans
Not that old - I'm only XX
Anyone for a bath?
Rome is a REPUBLIC. We got rid of our king 200 years ago...
Good riddance!
The Romans began to conquer other places ...
Let's start with the rest of Italy!
...and move on to everywhere else!
I hear North Africa is very nice
Lovely beaches!
And these are my elephants
I'm HANNIBAL leading the Carthaginians
Grrr
Brrr
ALPS
They had a huge fight on their hands with the city of CARTHAGE in North Africa ... But eventually Rome ruled most of the countries round the Mediterranean.

Meanwhile back in Rome...
Take that, greedy posh person!
Take that, lowly oik!
ouch!
ouch!
tension between rich and poor led to CIVIL WAR.
Then a Roman army general took control of Rome...
I'm SULLA
I'm in charge now!
HNNG!
And I'm not very nice
When he died there was a struggle for power...
BIFF
WHACK
BASH
OW
which was won by JULIUS CAESAR
glint glint
glint glint
ooh
He's so muscular!
But then...
URK
And there was more fighting until Rome got its first EMPEROR...

THE FALL OF THE ROMAN EMPIRE.

Hello... I'm Augustus Caesar, EMPEROR of Rome
All this is mine... all mine
CACKLE

Emperors came and went...

CALIGULA dressed as a goddess and made his horse a politician.
GLUG
Steady on!
He drank pearls dissolved in vinegar and generally was a mad, evil tyrant.

CLAUDIUS made a law allowing people to fart at dinner.
He died after he was fed poisoned mushrooms by his wife.

hnng!!
KILL!!
KILL!
KILL!!
froth froth
I think he's in one of his moods
NERO sentenced his first wife to death, killed his second wife and had his own mother murdered.

heh heh
COMMODUS fought as a gladiator. He always won because his opponents' weapons were made of lead.

ELAGABALUS held very extravagant dinner parties
rose petals
suffocated guests
URK
URK
URK

URK
VALERIAN was captured, killed and stuffed with straw by Persian king Shapur.

In their spare time... the Romans invented aqueducts, decent roads, central heating...
And horse shoes
Lucky for some.

The empire was at its biggest at the time of the Emperor HADRIAN ... a bit too big... then little bits dropped off here and there...
Whoops!
There goes another bit!

Then the empire was divided in two...

ROME
CONSTANTINOPLE

And the BARBARIANS arrived...

BARBARIANS!

Around 300 AD, the barbarian tribes outside the Roman Empire were on the move...
ANGLES & SAXONS
VANDALS*
restless
HUNS
WEST
VISIGOTHS
OSTROGOTHS
highly strung
FRANKS
ALANS
The Romans called all foreigners 'barbarians' (only in Latin)
Ooh the beasts!
OW
Yeah!
Not all of them were barbarous. But these tribes were pretty hard
The Goths probably did not look like this
shame
The Huns rampaged through Europe...
BIFF
mum!
aaaagh
hnn!
Ow! That was uncalled for!
BASH
The Goths scarpered into the Roman Empire
*And some of them are still around

A lot of rampaging went on...

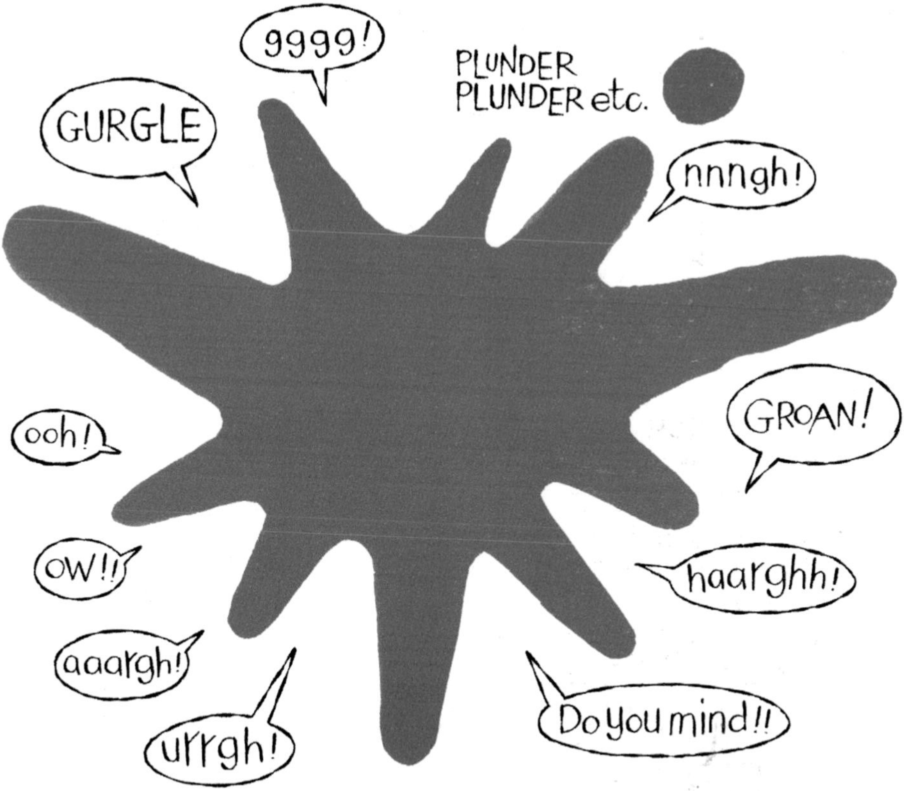
gggg!
PLUNDER
PLUNDER etc.
GURGLE
nnngh!
ooh!
GROAN!
OW!!
haarghh!
aaargh!
urrgh!
Do you mind!!

The barbarians eventually stopped rampaging and became the countries of Europe...
ANGLE
FRANK
ALAN
Plunder? No Way
Pillage? Forget it
BRITAIN
FRANCE
SPAIN
N.AFRICA
KEVIN
ROY
REMOTE
The kevins & Roys settled on a remote island in the North Sea where they died out (actually we just made that up)
In 476 AD barbarian leader Odoacer kicked out the last Western Roman Emperor...
pretty fed up
BIFF BIFF
ODY rules OK

The HUNs were the scariest barbarians of the lot...

Attila the Hun

The HUNS were especially famous for being ruthless, cruel MARAUDERS
Maim!
Hack!
Make a mess!
My name is ATTILA
hhhn
They call me the SCOURGE of GOD
They were skilled riders. Children learned to ride as soon as they could walk.
goo goo
hhhn
They were extremely handy with a BOW and ARROW...
ouch!
urk

A shepherd found a sword and gave it to Attila...
This proves it! I'm chosen by God to rule the WHOLE WORLD!
glint, froth etc.
hnn
Gold!!! Then we'll say goodbye
Oh all right. Here you are then
Attila led his army on a path of destruction across EUROPE. They besieged CONSTANTINOPLE (but agreed to leave for 3 TONNES of gold)
har har har
har har
nng
Mine, all mine
... and conquered huge chunks of what had been the Roman Empire.
But then...
urk
Attila died, probably after drinking too much and having a nasty NOSEBLEED.

At about the same time, over in the PACIFIC...

the POLYNESIANS

The POLYNESIANS lived on islands scattered about in the Pacific Ocean

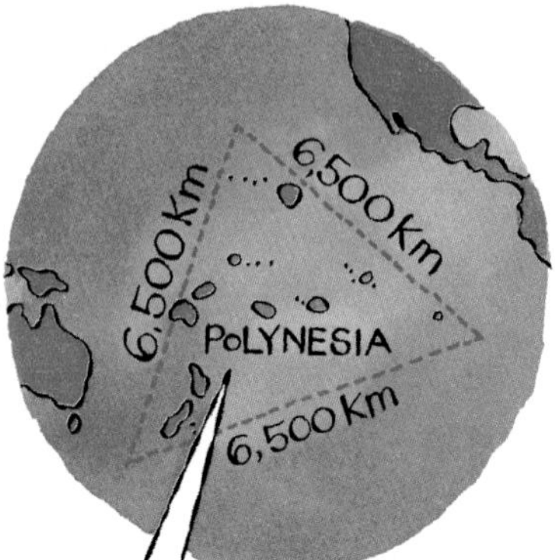
6,500 km
6,500 km
6,500 km
POLYNESIA

To reach these islands they made some amazing journeys ...
Just hope we've packed enough sandwiches

Originally from islands north of Australia...
AUSTRALIA
Are we nearly there yet?
they travelled further and further into the Pacific Ocean
They colonised EASTER ISLAND
Oh not more tourists
...and HAWAII
...and finally NEW ZEALAND
whew
While the Polynesians were travelling across thousands of kilometres of open sea...
sailors everywhere else in the world rarely went out of sight of land.
Aargh, me hearties! There be sea monsters out there!
Fancy a night in?

And now it was about time for...

The Dark Ages

In EUROPE...
Pass the turnips!
Things were a lot more civilised when the Romans were here...
SIGH
I'm cold... throw another book on the fire!

Elsewhere...

In the GUPTA empire in Northern India, brilliant mathematicians, astronomers and philosophers were at work
We invented the decimal system!
...and the number O
But...
the pesky Huns destroyed us in 500.
sums
more sums
Bother!
The MAYAN civilisation was the most powerful in the Americas
We have a written language
and lovely calendars like this
...and the odd bit of human sacrifice never hurt anyone.
heh heh

Back in EUROPE...
More turnips?
Will you STOP that!
YAWN
I wish the MIDDLE AGES would hurry up!

... and over in

Ch'ang-an, the capital of the TANG dynasty, was the biggest city in the world
Female Tang ruler Wu Zetian was the only Empress in Chinese history.
I'm the boss OK!
Our silk and porcelain are the best
Definitely
By about 850 the huge ISLAMIC empire included Spain, North Africa, Persia and Syria.
Massive!!
Our empire's bigger than the Roman Empire...
And we know loads about science...
But we don't like to brag...
much

Further north there was a lot of pillaging going on...

VIKINGS!
In the 700s...
Haaargh!
Viking longships set sail...
They started from here...
NORWAY
SWEDEN
DENMARK
(some walked)
and ended up all over the place.
We're looking for land to farm...
haaargh
and things to pillage
and slaves to capture
I'm just looking for trouble!
SLURP

They conquered lots of Britain...
HAAAAARGH
steady on!
and Ireland...
and sailed right across the Atlantic.
Some stayed in Iceland...
Phew!
and some in Greenland.
Land! GASP
But they didn't stay in North America
clear off!
oooh!
...the locals were too fierce.
Some Vikings were given land in France
They call us the NORMANS
Yeah!
(more on them later...)

And in the East it paid to be fierce too
(some were better at it than others)

MONGOLS
Over in Central Asia MONGOL tribes roamed the steppes.
They moved with their animals and lived in tents.
And sometimes...
Grrr
Nnngh!
different tribes fought each other.
Until...
Ghhh!
They call me GENGHIS KHAN
It means 'universal leader'
but I don't like to brag
GENGHIS united all the Mongol tribes...
Behave! Or else!
OW
and led his hordes on a path of destruction.
WHACK
SLICE
CHOP
URK
How dare you!!

Hhnn!
whinny
The Mongols were excellent riders
... deadly archers
snort
Look out it's the Mongol horde
Bother
... and ruthless conquerors
His empire grew and grew until...
URK
Genghis Khan died.
The empire passed to his sons
I'm OGUDAI. Now I'm the Great Khan.
heh heh
Ogudai conquered RUSSIA and HUNGARY. Then
URK
... he died too.
But the Mongols kept on conquering
I'm KUBLAI KHAN
I am Genghis Khan's grandson
and my empire is absolutely ENORMOUS.
EUROPE
ASIA
ARABIA
AFRICA
INDIA
Meanwhile, empires grew in other parts of the world...

The Moors in Spain

The huge Islamic empire had two capital cities...
CORDOBA
BAGHDAD
AFRICA
The Islamic conquerors of Spain, known as the MOORS, ruled most of Spain for hundreds of years.
That means he's in charge!
I'm the CALIPH
They brought wonderful new crops...
Orange, banana, apricot, fig?
Thanks, don't mind if I do!
and libraries, universities and hospitals.
I'm ABU al QASIM, top surgeon
Anyone for an op?
Cordoba was the most cultured city in Europe.
It's SO sophisticated!
and stripes are so NOW!
Eventually, the Christian rulers in the north of Spain united against the Moors...
gouge!
OW
shriek
That is so unfair!
urk
BIFF
King FERDINAND and Queen ISABELLA kicked the Moors out of their last stronghold, GRANADA, in 1492
...and STAY OUT!
And further south...

AFRICAN EMPIRES
The GHANA* empire in WEST AFRICA was the first of several empires in the area
here
AFRICA
*not to be confused with the present-day country of Ghana
The empire grew rich from...
GOLD, lovely gold!
until it was attacked by the Moors (yes, them again)
Then came the MALI empire. MANSA MUSA, its ruler, was amazingly rich. He had GOLD DUST scattered in front of him on a trip to Mecca.
Oi!
MECCA
Get sprinkling!
After 150 years or so the Mali empire was conquered by the SONGHAI
eek
BASH
ow
urk
Its capital TIMBUKTU was a centre of TRADE and LEARNING
Other parts of AFRICA had wealthy empires too...
Yes, just look at those ruins in GREAT ZIMBABWE
Extraordinary!
By the way, what was happening in Europe?

WAR!
(lots of it)
In 1066...
I'm King Harold and...
I'm WILLIAM... call me THE CONQUEROR
Haargh
har har
The NORMANS led by WILLIAM defeated English King HAROLD at the Battle of Hastings
I feel a RAMPAGE* coming on!
It must be my VIKING blood!
* He did a lot of that...
Meanwhile...
The city of JERUSALEM was a top religious destination for Christians and Muslims...
PILGRIMS THIS WAY
ooh
BIFF
URK
stop that!
OW
WHACK
It had been conquered by Turkish Muslims...
Yah!
It's a war!
And it's HOLY!
Everybody's happy!
So the Christian Pope called for a CRUSADE to kick them out.
Aaaagh
urk
BASH
hnn
That's not nice
ooh
The First Crusade captured Jerusalem.
But Muslim leader SALADIN recaptured the city in 1187.
It's mine now!
har har

The Crusades went on for 200 years or so...
grrr!
I'm getting really fed up with this!
urgh!
sigh
then everyone got bored and went home.
Crusading's all very well...
Not if you keep losing though
and it's a bit messy...
Mine's a pint
In the end Jerusalem was ruled by MUSLIMS
It's ours again heh heh
Go home infidel!
Meanwhile, a series of wars were fought between England and France...
BIFF
eek
urk
Bah!
Go 'ome rosbif!
Zut alors
mainly because kings of England thought they should be kings of France too...
It'll be called the HUNDRED YEARS WAR
Zis goes on for 116 Years!
aaargh
Luckily, we didn't know it lasted that long!
urk

And by the 14th century, a different kind of fever was sweeping Europe...

PLAGUE
The BLACK DEATH arrived in Europe...
Ooh I don't feel very...
ACHE
URK
JOINT ACHE
SWELLINGS
VOMIT
There were some unusual remedies...
Drink a mixture of eggshell, marigolds, treacle and beer.
nng
SQUAWK
Place a live HEN next to the swelling.
Drink your own pee twice a day.
I'd rather have a cup of tea
niffy
It won't hurt (much)
Soften the swellings with cooked onions and figs. Then CUT open the swellings.
Put a live FROG on the swelling.
croak
croak
stinky
Take a bath in human pee.
but they didn't work

The PLAGUE was spread by FLEAS
Yes, it was US!
heh heh
but no one at the time knew that
It's those cats and dogs!
COUGH COUGH
urk
Yeah! Kill them!
urk
I blame it on foreigners!
Yeah! Kill them!
Few people recovered from the plague
stench
Groan
moan
Sometimes the healthy were walled up with the sick. It killed between a third and half the population of Europe.

But not everyone was dying of plague...

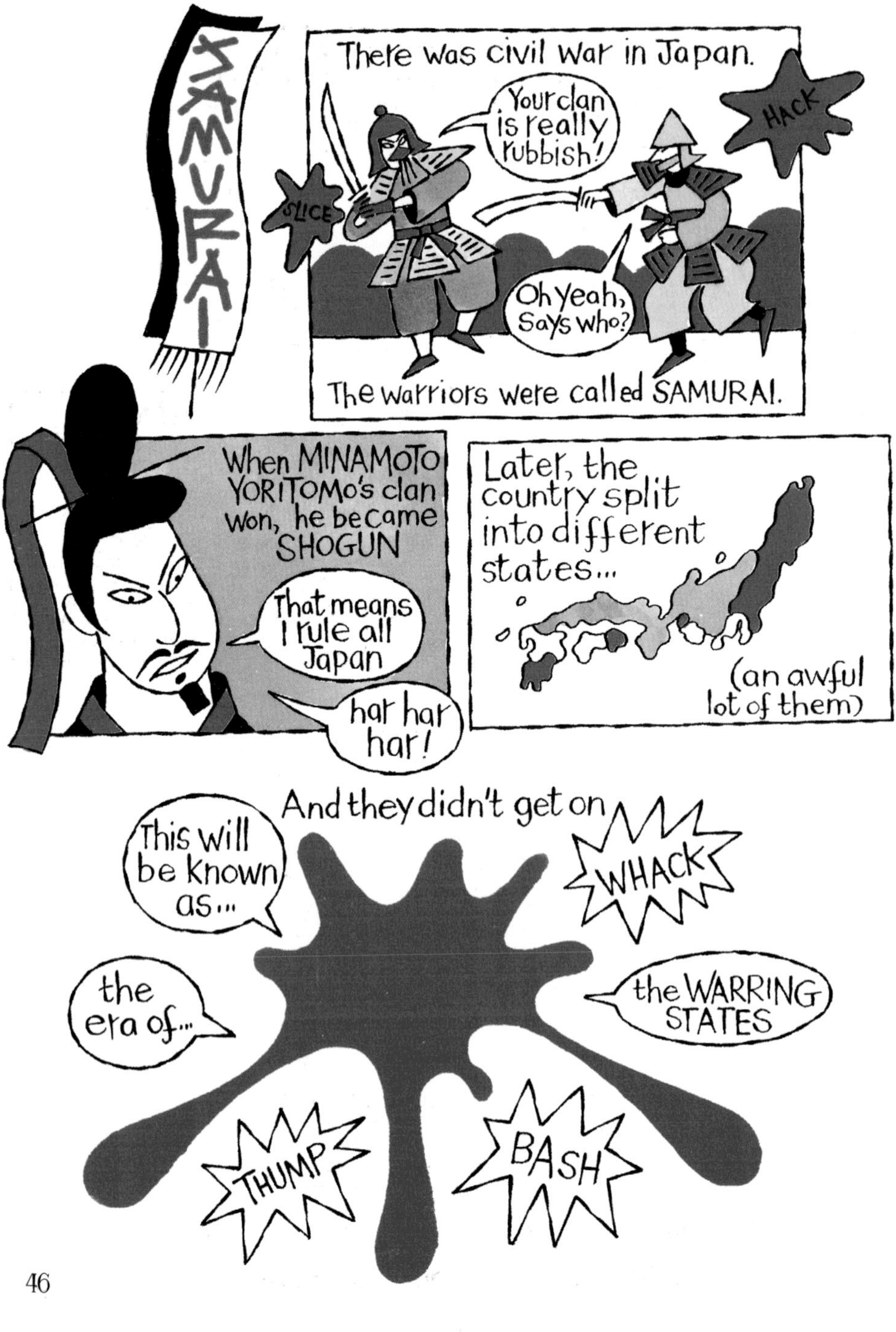
SAMURAI
There was civil war in Japan.
Your clan is really rubbish!
HACK
SLICE
Oh yeah, Says who?
The warriors were called SAMURAI.
When MINAMOTO YORITOMO's clan won, he became SHOGUN
That means I rule all Japan
har har har!
Later, the country split into different states...
(an awful lot of them)
And they didn't get on
This will be known as...
WHACK
the era of...
the WARRING STATES
THUMP
BASH

A samurai's most important weapon was the sword
GLINT GLEAM
Hnnn!
Other weapons were just as scary
JUTTE– nasty truncheon
TESSEN-metal fan for bashing
OOF
The samurai followed BUSHIDO, the way of the warrior, which sometimes meant...
I prefer honour to shame
So I'm going to do something messy
URK
After an awful lot of fighting, Japan was reunited
No hard feelings eh?
Finally, there was peace. Samurai didn't have much to do...
I'm thinking of a career in the civil service
I thought accountancy
After several centuries, the samurai class was abolished altogether.

Meanwhile, on the other side of the world, the set-up was a bit different...

ROYALS

EUROPE was divided into kingdoms. The English Tudors were a powerful bunch...

Henry VII was the first Tudor king of England.
That's me
Har har, that's the end of you, Richard III!
urk
Budge over!
Do you mind?
When he died, his son HENRY took over the job. He had lots of WIVES
...and chopped off lots of heads
hnng
nice
fed up
There's nothing like a good decapitation!
...two belonged to his wives.
nng
creak creak
codpiece
bad leg
Later, Henry was so ill and fat he needed a winch to get him out of bed.
urk
His son EDWARD didn't last long.
COUGH COUGH
urk
Henry's daughter MARY became Queen. She was a little ... er... strange.
Burn the Protestants!
roast them!
Burn!

Then Henry's other daughter became queen.
Hello there
Oh no! Not another feeble woman!
ELIZABETH I ruled for 45 years and defeated the SPANISH ARMADA (among other things)
Har har! Who's feeble now?

There were other powerful kings and queens in Europe

CHARLES V, Holy Roman Emperor, ruled over bits of Italy, Germany, the Netherlands, Sicily, Sardinia, Spain and the Americas
WHEW!
But my gout's killing me!
JOANNA the MAD ruled Spain with Charles
ooh
froth froth
cackle cackle
... but she wasn't much help.
After Charles and Joanna, PHILLIP II ruled Spain, the richest country in the world.
Hmm... might as well take over Portugal

...since we're so disgustingly rich!
har har

On the other side of the Atlantic...

AZTECS

TENOCHTITLAN, capital of the AZTEC empire, was one of the biggest cities on earth. 200,000 people lived there.
We've got a great view and a canal system too
the odd bit of human sacrifice
squelch
URK
Oops... make that 199,999 people
King FERDINAND and Queen ISABELLA, who ruled most of Spain, had some ideas
Now that we've got rid of those beastly Moors in our own country...
Let's invade someone else's!
heh heh
Columbus! Find us somewhere to conquer!
At once!
GULP

COLUMBUS arrived in the Americas in 1492. He landed in the West Indies.
At last!
More Europeans followed him. Spanish CONQUISTADOR Hernando CORTES was the first to arrive in Central America.
har har
Mexico!!
I hear there's good PLUNDERING to be had in these parts
Aztec emperor MONTEZUMA welcomed him ...
Hello there
Nice weather
But...
Yikes
Get off!
URK
OW
har har
It's ours now!
The Spanish captured TENOCHTITLAN and the whole Aztec empire.
new!
ATLANTIC
PACIFIC
Cortes now ruled 'NEW SPAIN'
...which was a lot bigger than Old Spain.
old
ATLANTIC OCEAN
AFRICA

It wasn't long before they started eyeing up South America too ...

INCAS

The INCA empire was vast. It ruled over 12 million people...
We've got some amazing ARCHITECTURE up here
Yes, don't the stones fit together a treat?
Love your feathers, by the way!
clever terraced farming
squelch
human sacrifice
...again
The Incas made beautiful GOLD and SILVER objects...
INGOT
INGOT
INGOT
INGOT
(Most of it was melted down by the SPANISH)
They even practised BRAIN SURGERY
This won't hurt (much)
Then...
aargh
urk
FRANCISCO PIZARRO arrived...
ATAHUALPA, the Incan emperor, welcomed him*
I smell TREASURE!
TWITCH TWITCH
nng!
Er... hello
Come with US, Inca!
Get off!

*Does all this sound familiar ??

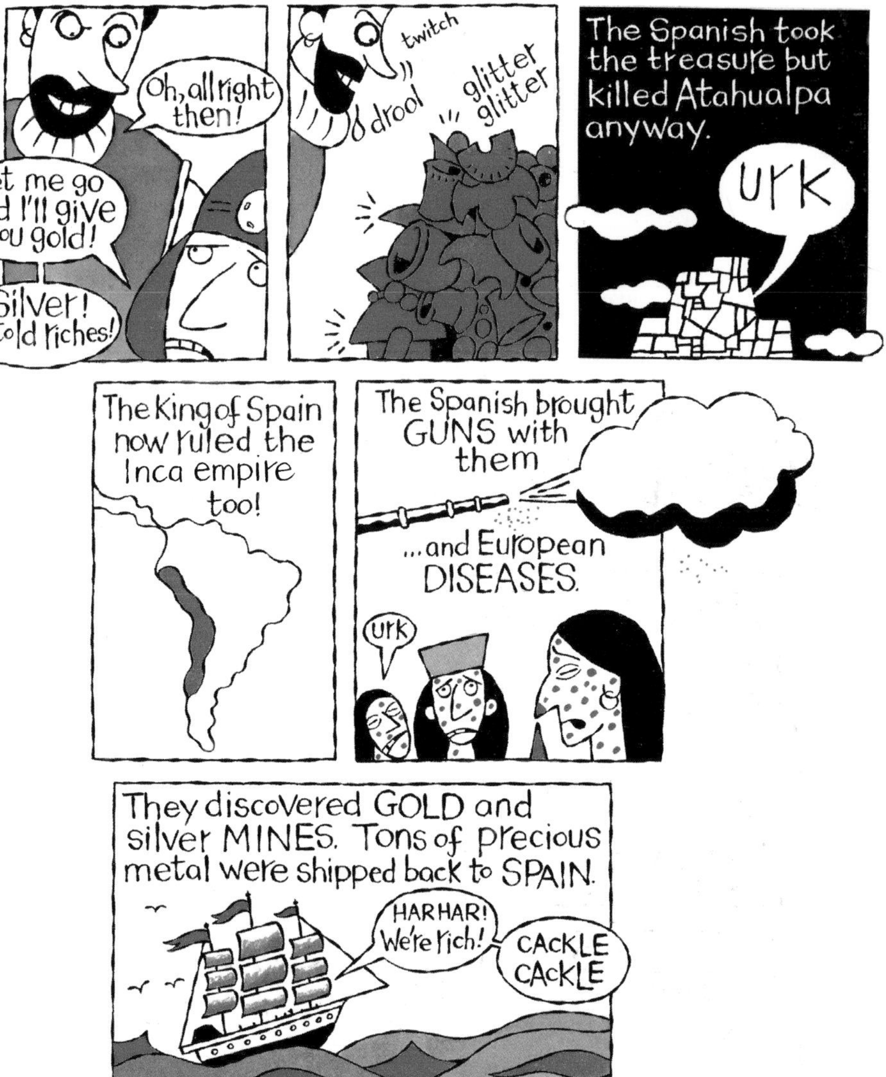
Let me go and I'll give you gold!
Silver! Untold riches!
Oh, all right then!
twitch
drool
glitter glitter
The Spanish took the treasure but killed Atahualpa anyway.
URK
The King of Spain now ruled the Inca empire too!
The Spanish brought GUNS with them
...and European DISEASES.
URK
They discovered GOLD and silver MINES. Tons of precious metal were shipped back to SPAIN.
HAR HAR! We're rich!
CACKLE CACKLE

Meanwhile, on the other side of the world...

Moghuls

BABUR was the first MOGHUL emperor.
My name means, 'TIGER'
GRRR Heh heh
He was descended from MONGOL conquerers...
And I'm about to do some conquering of my own!
He began by conquering AFGHANISTAN
urk
ow
screech
Then...
Right, let's start on INDIA
Har har
He led his ARMY through the mountains...
Come on, keep up!
to the plains of PANIPAT
POW
BOOM
Pooh to you, Indian army from DELHI!
We may be outnumbered, but we have GUNS!
uh oh!
I just hate loud noises!
Babur won the battle.

AKBAR, Babur's grandson, did even more conquering...
More! I want more!
Hnnn
AKBAR'S EMPIRE
ARABIAN SEA
He built FATEHPUR SIKRI (it means 'City of Victory')
...and had 300 wives
He never remembers our anniversary
Akbar had fierce opponents...
Hnn
Hnnn!
We're the fierce RAJPUTS of north-west India
but the empire was mostly peaceful.
hmm
We all rub along quite well really...
Until...
urk

Akbar's grandson was SHAH JAHAN
It means 'King of the World'
but I don't like to brag
Things weren't so peaceful...
There's not much money left, either, which is a shame
...because I like spending it!
TOIL TOIL
And we work hard for it!
Shah Jahan had a favourite wife, called MUMTAZ
She died and Shah Jahan's heart was broken...
SOB
BOO HOO
so he built her a modest little tomb.

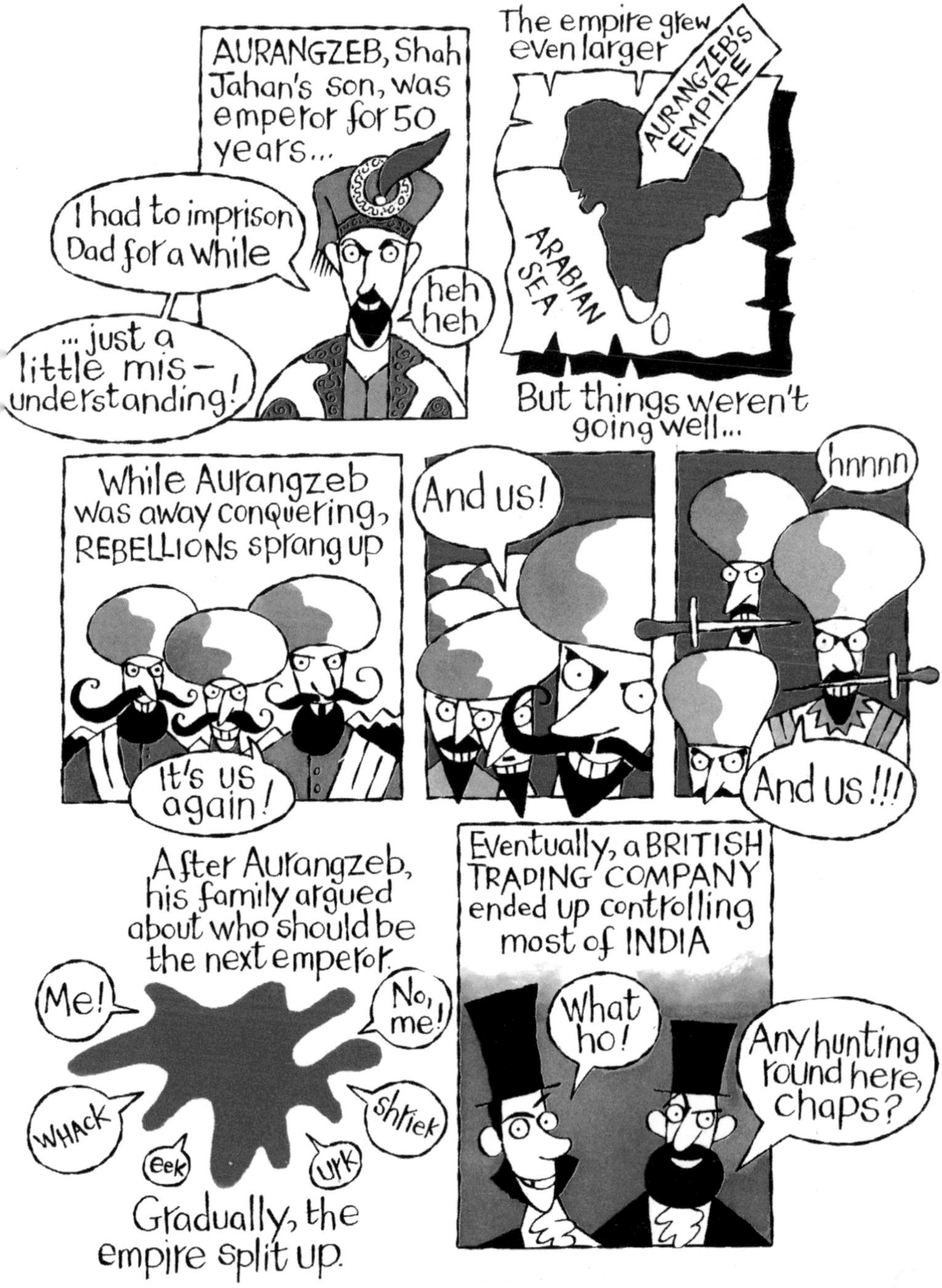
AURANGZEB, Shah Jahan's son, was emperor for 50 years...
I had to imprison Dad for a while
... just a little mis-understanding!
heh heh
The empire grew even larger
AURANGZEB'S EMPIRE
ARABIAN SEA
But things weren't going well...
While Aurangzeb was away conquering, REBELLIONS sprang up
It's us again!
And us!
hnnnn
And us!!!
After Aurangzeb, his family argued about who should be the next emperor.
Me!
No, me!
WHACK
eek
urk
shriek
Gradually, the empire split up.
Eventually, a BRITISH TRADING COMPANY ended up controlling most of INDIA
What ho!
Any hunting round here, chaps?

China was a slightly different cup of tea...

MING
CHINA was part of the MONGOL empire until...
The peasants are revolting!
That's already an old joke and it's 1368!
A peasant leader became the first MING Emperor of an independent China.
It's time for a few changes
...but first, peel me a grape!
The Ming dynasty lasted for more than 300 years.
Life improved for the peasants...
Thanks Ming!
China grew rich from foreign trade
Nice cup of tea!
SLURP
SLURP
PORCELAIN
SILK

A GREAT WALL—yes, another one—was built to keep out northern invaders. (This one is still there.)

The FORBIDDEN CITY in Beijing was the IMPERIAL COURT
Apart from the Emperor, his family and imperial officials, no one was allowed to enter–the punishment was DEATH
I only wanted a quick look!
During the Ming era, Chinese explorers sailed as far as southern Africa.
Are we nearly there yet?
Some people think they sailed even further...
Weird!
Later, foreign voyages were banned
In the 1600s things started going wrong and the Ming dynasty weakened.
Bribe me I'm an official!
And I'm feeling rebellious!
heh heh
Eventually, people from the north did conquer China (the Great Wall hadn't worked after all) and a new dynasty took over...
We are the QING, aka the mean MANCHU
nnng
Then, shock horror...

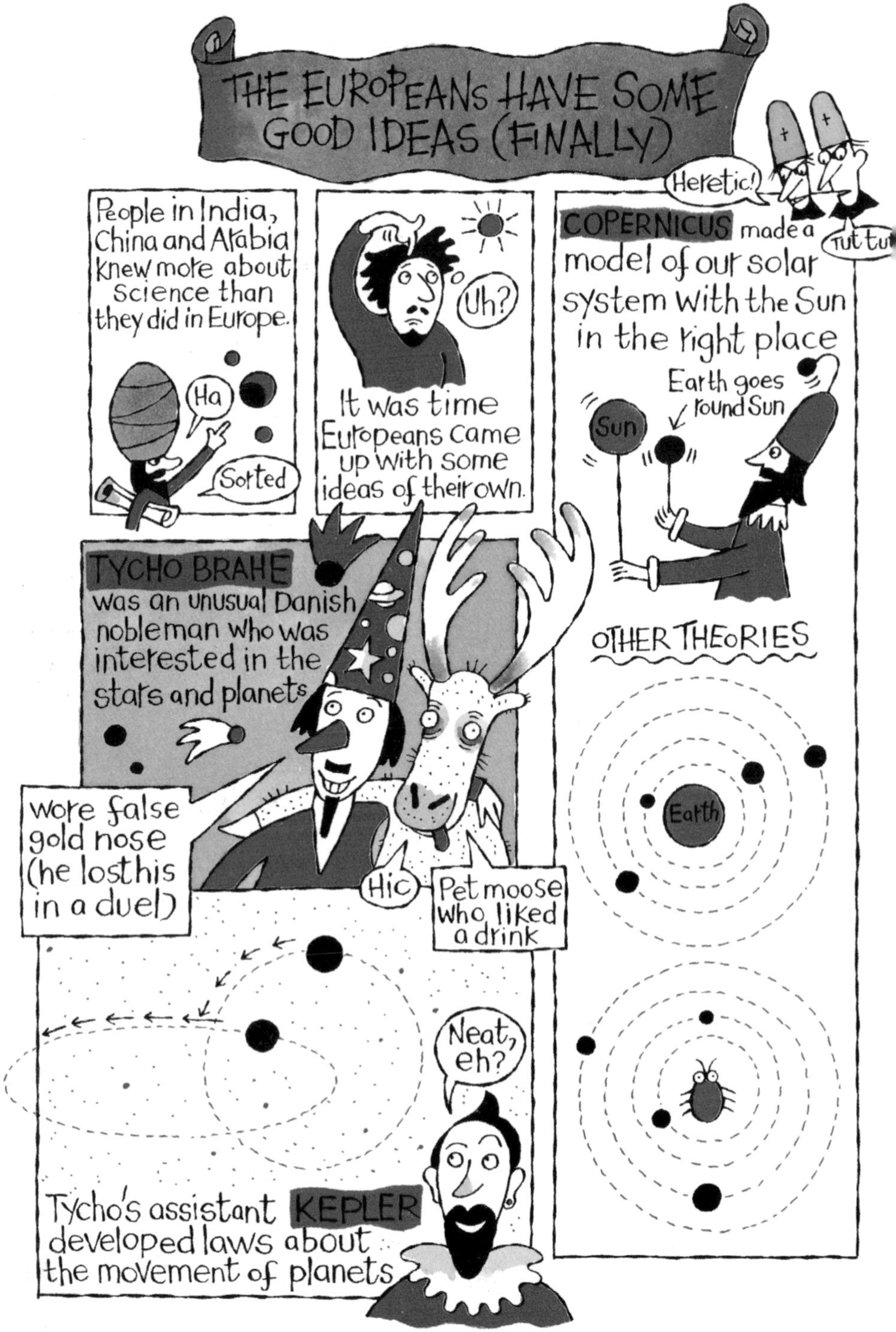
THE EUROPEANS HAVE SOME GOOD IDEAS (FINALLY)
People in India, China and Arabia knew more about science than they did in Europe.
Ha
Sorted
Uh?
It was time Europeans came up with some ideas of their own.
Heretic!
Tut tut
COPERNICUS made a model of our solar system with the Sun in the right place
Earth goes round Sun
Sun
TYCHO BRAHE was an unusual Danish nobleman who was interested in the stars and planets
wore false gold nose (he lost his in a duel)
Hic
Pet moose who liked a drink
OTHER THEORIES
Earth
Neat, eh?
Tycho's assistant KEPLER developed laws about the movement of planets

GALILEO improved the design of the telescope and used it to look at the night sky. He had lots of clever thoughts.
Yes, the Earth definitely orbits the Sun!
Wow... Jupiter has LOTS of moons
He also invented the thermometer.
mmm!
Time for a cup of tea
OUCH!!
Er... gravity affects objects on Earth and planets in space!
NEWTON was struck by an idea about gravity
HARVEY discovered how blood circulates through the body.
Goodgrief!
WHAT HE SAW
germy
titchy
LEEUWENHOEK discovered bacteria, blood corpuscles and other tiny things using a microscope.

Other Europeans were discovering much bigger things...

Explorers
The Chinese had already done some exploring of their own. Suddenly, the Europeans were at it...
The English and French both tried to get to Asia by sailing North. Lots of them froze to death.
Hmm... that's a bit odd!
I know! The world must be pear-shaped!
CHRISTOPHER COLUMBUS sailed to the West Indies. He thought he had arrived in India.
a bit boring
Hello, sailor
monsters
scary stuff
VASCO da GAMA sailed round Africa to India, upsetting all sorts of people along the way
adventur
I like to EXPLORE
and I like being NASTY
OW
ooh

LIFE ON BOARD SHIP
Sailors had hardly any fresh fruit and veg so lots of them got SCURVY
mumble mumble
but there was plenty of HARD TACK
BISCUIT
WEEVILS
... and RATS
surprise!
WATER kept in wooden barrels often went bad
STENCH
So instead they drank BEER – 16th century sailors in the English Navy had a ration of 4.5 litres a day.
hic
ZZZ
FERDINAND MAGELLAN led the first ever ROUND-THE-WORLD voyage
Aren't I clever?
but... OUCH
Unfortunately he was chopped to bits on the way.
CAPTAIN JAMES COOK mapped Australia, New Zealand and some of the Pacific islands in the 18th century.
Er... thanks
He was killed by Hawaiians, who kindly gave some of his remains to his crew.
unknown

There was plenty to be afraid of at sea, not least...

Pirates!

Thieving cut-throats roamed the high seas in the 1600s and 1700s, striking terror (and cutlasses) into the hearts of their victims.

Ye swab
Arrr
Avast there!
Arrr etc.
Scurvy dogs!
Where's me grog?
Cup o'tea anyone?
Some rather unpleasant pirate punishments
Jolly Roger
Drinking from the yard arm
bleh!
Cat-o'nine-tails
ooh
Walking the plank
Shan't
Marooning
Come back!
Keel hauling
ouch
Davy Jones' locker

RACHEL WALL ran away from home to become a pirate.
So there
I'm off!
sea biscuit
She survived a shipwreck but was later hanged.
URK
BLACK BART captured more than 400 ships in his short career.
heh!
400
MARY READ and ANNE BONNY dressed as men and terrorised the Caribbean seas with their pirate partner CALICO JACK.
Be afraid, matey
Belay, me earties... and mind me hairstyle!
Haargh!
The notorious BLACKBEARD marooned 17 of his crew and shot his first mate.
He was killed by the British Navy and his head was stuck on their ship's prow.
RUM 'N' GUN-POWDER
favourite drink
CAPTAIN KIDD was hanged for piracy and murder of a shipmate. His body was covered in tar as a warning to others.
Some Pirate talk
Mm... lovely bumboo*
ZZZ
ZZZ
Snap!
Avast there, ye hornswaggler†
* Drink made from rum, nutmeg and sugar.
† Stop that, you cheat!

Many of these pirates plundered the coast of America...

US SETTLERS

In 1607, Europeans founded their first COLONY in AMERICA.
Where's the nearest hostelry?
Funny headgear!
There was plenty of room for the new SETTLERS and NATIVE AMERICANS
The settlers would have starved to death
GROAN
It's not like Plymouth
... if the Native Americans hadn't helped them.
No... eat it!
Nice day
Not bad
There were lots of different groups of Native Americans but most of them got on with the settlers.
Until... in 1675 a chief called METACOM was peeved with the settlers of New Hampshire.
These settlers are stealing all my land
I've had enough of this!
Keep out!
snarl
BIFF
WHACK
OW
eek
URK

So the settlers took their REVENGE...
urk
ow
uh
nng
aar
URK
Metacom was killed. His head ended up on a pole... where it stayed for 25 years. The Native Americans weren't quite so friendly after that...
In the south, settlers grew rich from crops like TOBACCO and SUGAR
HACK HACK
ECK ECK
Different colonies of settlers got together and became the UNITED STATES of AMERICA.
ATLANTIC OCEAN
Later, they became an independent country (after a bit of a fight known as the WAR of AMERICAN INDEPENDENCE)
By 1770 the NEW WORLD relied on a TERRIBLE TRADE
COTTON
SUGAR
EUROPE
Traded goods for SLAVES
AMERICA
Heh heh! Now you can work on my PLANTATION!
I'm not that keen actually
AFRICA
A few years later another revolution was brewing...

The French Revolution
Thought I'd wear something simple today...
SIMPER
The French king, LOUIS XVI, lived in luxury at his huge palace in VERSAILLES.
Meanwhile, in Paris...
I'm starving!
I could murder a bit of baguette...
Or an aristocrat!
Ordinary people declared themselves a NATIONAL ASSEMBLY.
Down with the GOVERNMENT!
Down with the KING!
nng
Liberty!
Equality?
Brotherhood!
Oi! What about sisterhood?
Let's storm the BASTILLE!
And nick all the ammunition!
Yeah!
The Storming of the Bastille marked the beginning of the FRENCH REVOLUTION.
SHRIEK
Haargh!
urk
urk

A group of women marched on the palace at Versailles
Kill the royal Parasites!
aarh!
Kill!
Soon France became a REPUBLIC.
Down with Poshos!
Chop off their heads!
A lawyer called ROBESPIERRE led the government for a short but GRUESOME time
...known as THE TERROR. Tens of thousands were executed, including the King and Queen.
Off with their heads!
Nnnnng!
A head-chopping machine made things very efficient ... but a bit messy.
Robespierre didn't last long...
At last a general called NAPOLEON BONAPARTE took control of FRANCE.
Hnn!
The rest of Europe was worried...

Especially the posh people.
Gosh, it couldn't happen here, could it?
Equal rights for everyone-even grubby peasants? Surely not!
We're not worried!
Vive la Révolution!
Yeah
Meanwhile...
Let's get CONQUERING!
Haaargh
BASH
BIFF
URK
The FRENCH EMPIRE grew.
Napoleon was made Emperor of France in 1804.
ENGLAND and FRANCE were at war. Napoleon had 180,000 troops ready to invade England.
Be afraid, Rosbifs!
nng
At the BATTLE of TRAFALGAR, British hero LORD NELSON defeated Napoleon at sea.
BOOM!
urk
KAPOW
ouch
Take that, Frenchie!
URK

But the NAPOLEONIC WARS continued on land. Napoleon made a bit of a mistake when he invaded RUSSIA ...
Retreat!
urk
brrr!
urk
Half a million French troops died on the way home. THEN...
I'm the DUKE of WELLINGTON!
I'm the leader of the BRITISH ARMY.
Har har!
They call me the IRON DUKE ...because I'm really, really hard!
Napoleon was defeated at the BATTLE of WATERLOO.
GERMAN troops
BELGIAN troops
urk
urk
DUKE of WELLINGTON leads the BRITISH
Tally Ho!
NAPOLEON leads the FRENCH
Zut!
DUTCH troops
PRUSSIAN troops
Napoleon was imprisoned by the British...
Got you!
hnn
Pah! There's no room to strut on this island!
then exiled to the island of St Helena...
where he died in 1821.
urk

The Brits soon had a revolution of their own...

INDUSTRIAL REVOLUTION

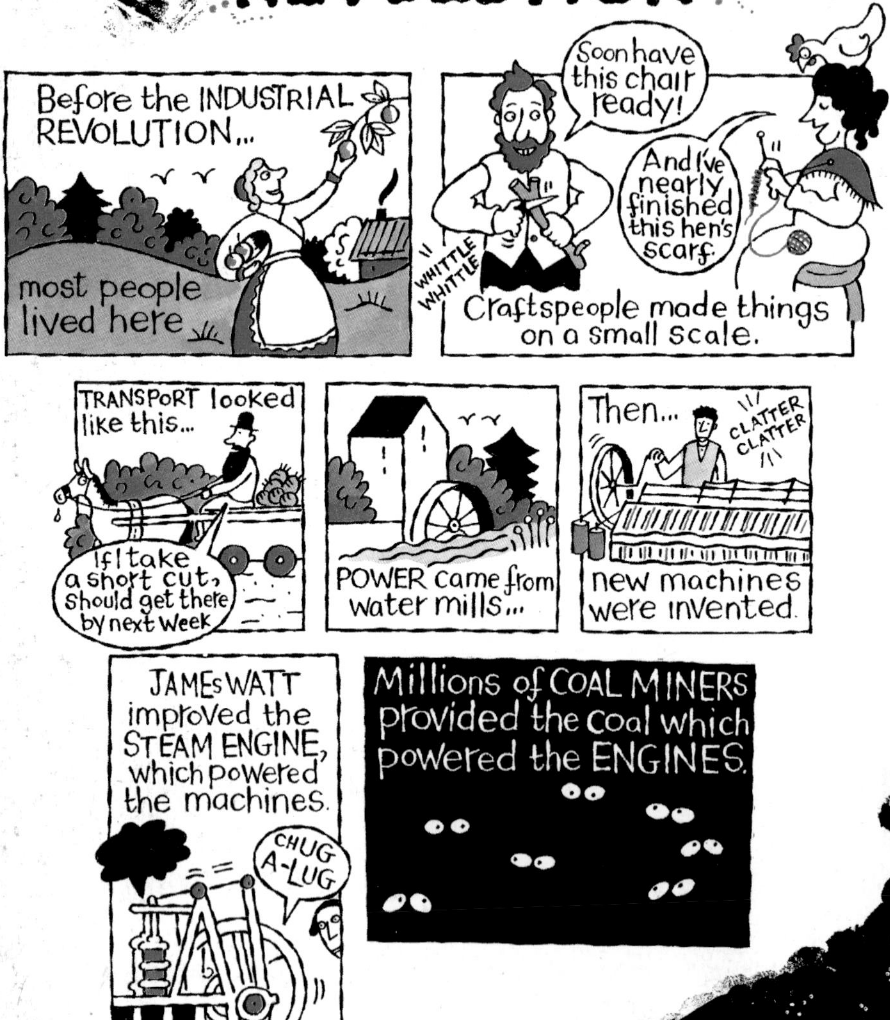

Before the INDUSTRIAL REVOLUTION...
most people lived here
Soon have this chair ready!
And I've nearly finished this hen's scarf.
WHITTLE WHITTLE
Craftspeople made things on a small scale.
TRANSPORT looked like this...
If I take a short cut, should get there by next week
POWER came from water mills...
Then...
CLATTER CLATTER
new machines were invented.
JAMES WATT improved the STEAM ENGINE, which powered the machines.
CHUG A-LUG
Millions of COAL MINERS provided the coal which powered the ENGINES.

GEORGE STEVENSON invented a faster way of moving things about.
GASP! 12 mph!!
It's not natural!
Factory owners grew rich
heh heh
Stop whining! You're getting a tea break next Tuesday, aren't you?
COUGH COUGH
...factory workers didn't.
For most of the 19th century, BRITAIN led the Industrial Revolution, and its empire got bigger and bigger...

The British Empire
I'm in charge!
Hurrah!
So there!
the whole of CANADA
lots of the WEST INDIES
...and this
ooh
Gosh, aren't we marvellous?
heh heh
It's our duty to civilise other countries
...and get very rich while we're at it!

The British Empire was enormous – the biggest there's ever been before or since. But not everyone was keen on top hats and teacakes...

They didn't bother with this bit!
I say!
all of INDIA
and lots more besides
lots of these bits too
and AUSTRALIA and NEW ZEALAND
Anyone for cricket?
Vast chunks of AFRICA
what about that bit?
That could do with a spot of civilising!

the rest of the NINETEENTH century
Fine figure of a woman!
Charming tea party!
Yes, we're taking tea outside today
...as we've got boys up the chimneys at the moment. So messy!
Ooh, my corset's killing me.
While the Victorians were taking tea
...in AUSTRALIA the locals were receiving some unexpected visitors.
Get a move on, vile wrongdoers!
I only stole some bread AND it was stale!
I want my mum!
They've got some very odd customs!
TRANSPORTATION to Australia as a punishment reached its peak around the 1830s.
There was CIVIL WAR in AMERICA when the southern states tried to leave the Union...
BIFF
eek
OW
Take that, southern losers!
BASH
urk
After four years of fighting, the northern states won. SLAVERY was abolished during the CIVIL WAR.
It's ours!
No, ours!
In CHINA there were OPIUM WARS...
In IRELAND there was a POTATO FAMINE...
shrivel
shrivel
Until 1854, foreigners weren't allowed into JAPAN and JAPANESE people weren't allowed out. Then...
Ooh, nice!
Travel Agents
trips to JAPAN!

There were lots of handy inventions in the 19th century...

Time for another revolution...

the RUSSIAN REVOLUTION

At the beginning of the 20th century, RUSSIA was ruled by TSAR NICHOLAS
I'm the Tsar. I'm in charge.
har har
fed up
The Tsar's troops shot a group of starving workers who went to him for help.
Help us, your Imperialness!
URK
People were still hungry... now they were ANGRY too.
In 1917...
Down with the Tsar!
The FEBRUARY REVOLUTION forced the Tsar to resign.
A few months later, the BOLSHEVIKS took charge.
I'm VLADIMIR LENIN. I may be a baldy but I'm the Bolshevik leader.
nng
You Red or White?
boom
BASH
Er...
URK
BIFF
The Bolshevik RED ARMY fought the WHITE ARMY, which included supporters of the Tsar and anti-Bolshevik troops from other countries.
The Bolsheviks made sure the Tsar never ruled again...
URK

Won the war with the Whites...
Biff
eek
urk
REDS rule OK
and changed their name.
Call us the COMMUNISTS! And the Russian Empire is now the UNION of SOVIET SOCIALIST REPUBLICS
ahem
USSR for short!
None of your la-di-da dukes and duchesses
And definitely no tsars!
everyone's a COMRADE now!
They made a few other changes too...
Men and women were given EQUAL RIGHTS.
Morning, Comrade.
Morning, Comrade
WORKERS had better rights and conditions
Hmm... Is there a catch?
The COMMUNIST PARTY was the only party allowed in RUSSIA...
And there isn't any jelly or icecream.
Then... Lenin died.
embalmed
His BRAIN was removed so it could be examined and prove that he was a genius.
JOSEPH STALIN became leader of the Communist Party...
hnnnn
nng

Meanwhile, in the rest of the world...

The TWENTIETH century was about to make its mark...
MEXICO had a revolution of its own.
BIFF
OW
URK
URK
In SARAJEVO in 1914
BANG
Take that, Archduke Franz Ferdinand!
URK
...which started the FIRST WORLD WAR
... which killed 15 MILLION people
URK
aargh
BOOM
BOOM
Then the FLU killed even more.
There was a REBELLION in IRELAND
Buzz off, Brits!
... 5 years later Ireland got its own government.
The 1920s were fun for some
I say!
... but not for others.
WE WANT WORK
There was CIVIL WAR in SPAIN.
har har
I'm FRANCO and I won!
... and another one in GERMANY.
The 1930s were grim for almost everyone.
I'm depressed
It's the GREAT DEPRESSION.
Me too.
SIGH
Groan
hnn
I'm a nasty NAZI!
Hey! I'm MUSSOLINI. Do as I say! Now!
There was also a FASCIST DICTATOR in ITALY
nnng
Let's invade POLAND!

The SECOND WORLD WAR went on for 6 years.
BooM
aargh
urk
urk
aaaargh
Millions died in NAZI DEATH CAMPS.
The war ended with a new kind of BOMB.
The new state of ISRAEL was created in PALESTINE
Oi! Hold on! We live here!
...which caused a few problems.
In INDIA, GANDHI led a PEACEFUL PROTEST for years
QUIT INDIA!
No biffing!
...until India finally became INDEPENDENT from Britain.
INDIA was divided in two
PAKISTAN
INDIA
...which also caused a few problems.
The COLONIES of the old European countries became INDEPENDENT.
Hurray!
About time too!
There was a REVOLUTION in CHINA
I'm MAO
Let's have a COMMUNIST CHINA!
I'm in charge!
Two groups of nations, one led by the SOVIET UNION, and the other by the USA, had a COLD WAR.
We're not actually FIGHTING
But we're very HUFFY with one another.
There was a lot of RIVALRY
WE put the first HUMANS in SPACE!
Well, WE landed on the MOON!
So poo to you!
USSR
USA
...but no more WORLD WARS.

CHINA suffered a terrible FAMINE
urk
urk
urk
BIFF
urk
urk
There was a WAR in VIETNAM (the USA was defeated for the first time ever)
...and another one between IRAN and IRA
aargh
PoW
eek
urk
...and other wars too.
On the PLUS side, WOMEN campaigned for EQUAL RIGHTS
Women can VOTE in most countries
But we still end up doing all the ironing!
In the USA, people campaigned for RACIAL EQUALITY
I have a dream...
You are our hero, MARTIN LUTHER KING!
And things did get better...
The SOVIET UNION broke up and in 1989 the BERLIN WALL came down.
Now we can go where we like
...and become CAPITALIST
I just want t bash a w down
heh heh
Eventually, the first MULTI-RACIAL elections were held in SOUTH AFRICA
And I won! Hooray!
Hooray!
MANDELA we love you!
Nice shirt Nelson!
The 21st CENTURY had a bad start. In 2003 the USA and other countries invaded IRAQ.
argh
PoW
urk
urk
And there are still a few problems to solve...
Maybe I should get rid of my 4x4?
NOW, how are we goin to stop the Ear OVERHEATIN
...the POLES melting
...and even more species DYING OUT?
urk

But look on the bright side! We've invented some interesting stuff...
aeroplane
nylon
mobile phone
I'm on the train.
dunk dunk
tea bag
space flight
ball-point pen
organ transplant
thud thud
MP3 player
penicillin
television
Hi there
Hi there
cloning
internet
munch munch
frozen food
tap tap
computer
... and who knows what we'll invent in the FUTURE?
Come back! You are my only friend!
Nothing wrong with a bit of GENETIC ENGINEERING!
CACKLE CACKLE

and now for **part two . . .**

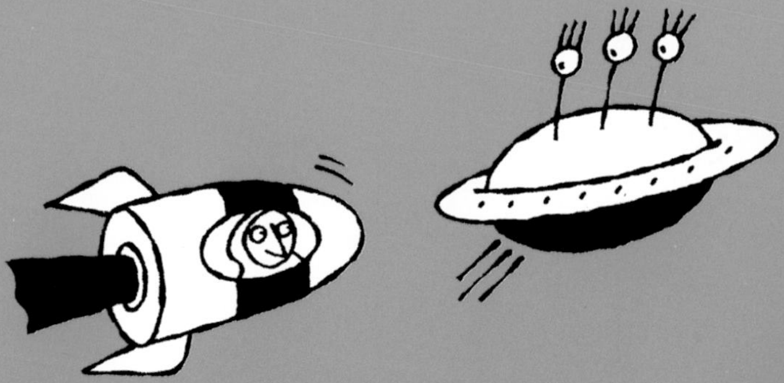

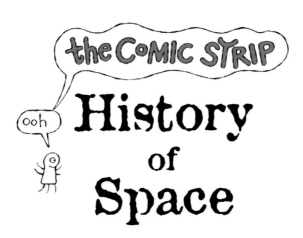

the COMIC STRIP History of Space

Contents

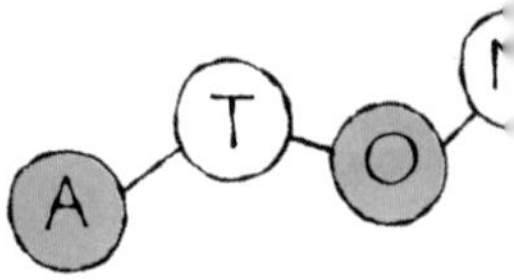

In the Beginning ...	1
Ka-boom!	2
Big Bang Theory	4
Atoms!	6
A Star is Born ...	8
Supernovas	10
The Sun	12
Our Solar System	14
Planet Earth	18
Life on Earth	20
Prehistoric People Look Up and Get Curious	22
Ancient Thoughts	24
The Ancient Babylonians	26
Constellations	28
Ancient Chinese Ideas	30
Ancient Egyptian Ideas	32
Ancient Greek Thoughts	34
Dark Age Astronomers	36
Copernicus	38
Kepler, Brahe (and Moose)	40
Galileo	42

Huygens 43
Telescopes 44
Newton 46
Comets! 48
New Planets 50
Space Stories 52
Einstein 54
Speeding Galaxies 56
Other Solar Systems 58
Close Encounters 60
Space Race 62
Animals in Space 64
Yuri Gagarin 66
Moon Landings 68
1st in Space 70
Black Holes, Quasars and Pulsars 72
Space Probes 74
Space Stations 76
Living in Space 78
To Infinity ... 80
and Beyond ... 82

IN THE BEGINNING...
Who knows? There are plenty of theories though...
absolutely NOTHING
or
BIFF
BUMP
BASH
A parallel Universe bumped into ours.
Or, an all-powerful GOD created everything.
(There are many different versions of him/her/it.)
Oooh, I know!
TWIDDLE TWIDDLE
Woooo
Krk!
or
A cosmic egg hatched.
Nnn
God being born
or maybe
The SKYWOMAN fell on to a GIANT TORTOISE.
Ooh, sorry!
Oi!
Then (probably)...

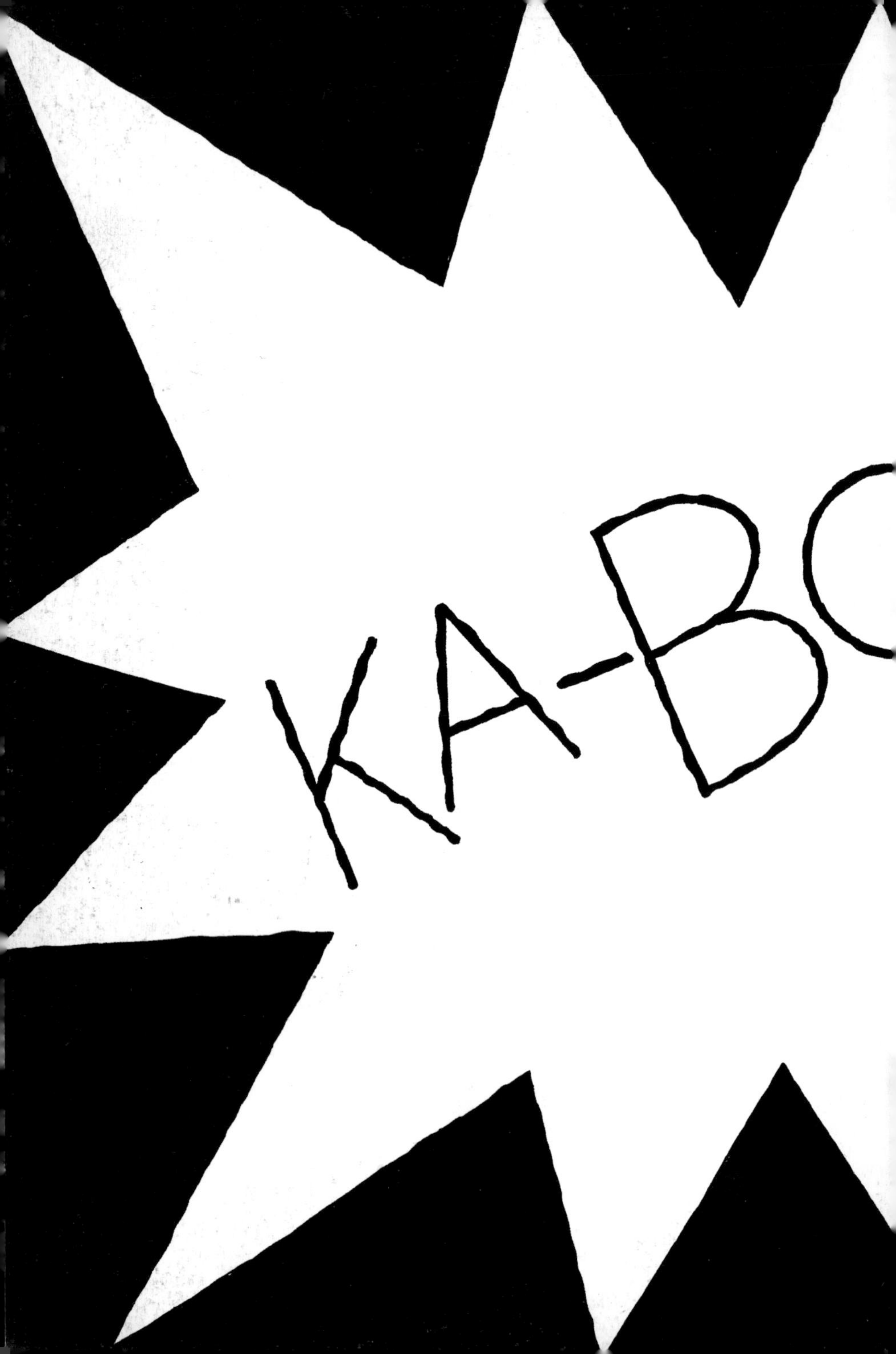
KA-BO

OM!

BIG BANG THEORY

In 1927, a priest called GEORGE LEMAÎTRE was studying astronomy...

Now just about everyone accepts BIG BANG theory. It says...

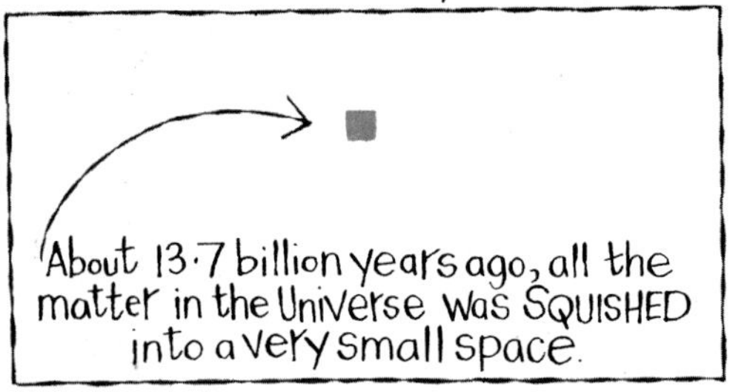
About 13·7 billion years ago, all the matter in the Universe was SQUISHED into a very small space.

It was incredibly HOT
and incredibly DENSE. Lots of stuff – EVERYTHING actually – packed in here

Then it exploded, E–X–P–A–N–D–I–N–G outwards...

Some modern scientists think the Big Bang wasn't the start of the Universe, but one of a series of BIG BOUNCES.
In fact there could be MANY Universes
... and eleven DIMENSIONS
I feel SICK!
we need more research into STRING THEORY
and LOOP QUANTUM GRAVITY.
Don't ask...
BOING
BOING

Either way, today's scientists think this is what happened after the Big Bang (or Bounce).

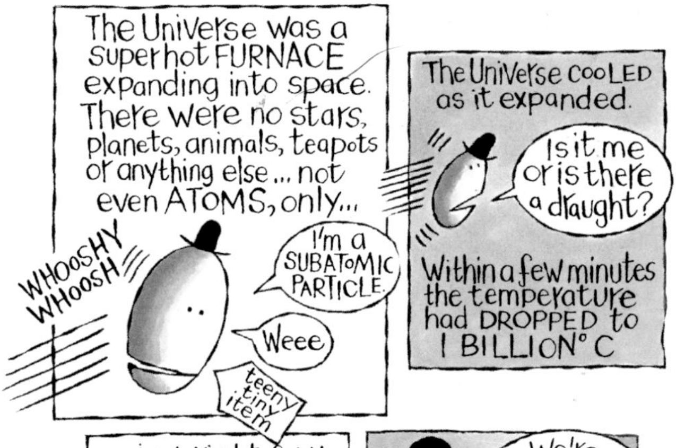
The Universe was a superhot FURNACE expanding into space. There were no stars, planets, animals, teapots or anything else ... not even ATOMS, only...
WHOOSHY WHOOSH
I'm a SUBATOMIC PARTICLE.
Weee
teeny tiny item
The Universe COOLED as it expanded.
Is it me or is there a draught?
Within a few minutes the temperature had DROPPED to 1 BILLION° C

... just right for the NUCLEI of the very first chemical ELEMENTS to form
I'm a HELIUM nucleus and I arrived next
I'm a HYDROGEN nucleus and I was here first!
... and I'm less common.
We're actually made up of smaller particles called PROTONS and NEUTRONS.
How many or few of them we have
...is what makes US different.

And then, about 300,000 years after the Big Bang...

ATOMS!

The Universe cooled down enough for ATOMS to form.

The nuclei were a bit useless on their own, so they met up with electrons and became ATOMS.
Hi... I'm an ELECTRON.
And I'm irresistibly drawn to you.
We give things structure. Without us there wouldn't be any THINGS at all.
And we allow LIGHT to travel. Without us everything would be DARK.
Ooh... I'd go weak at the knees if I had any!
GULP!

I just love all this attention!
Now we're an ATOM!

EVERYTHING is made of atoms. Without atoms the Universe would be clouds of particles. and nothing else.

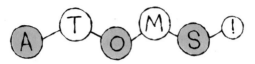

We now know there ARE smaller things than atoms, as we've already seen: electrons
... the nucleus of the atom
... the protons and neutrons
and even these are made of really teeny particles called QUARKS.
That's as far as we've got at the moment
... but we might find even TITCHIER things in the future.
For example, STRING THEORY suggests there are teeny weeny weeny loops of VIBRATING STRING.

Apart from hydrogen and helium, nothing else existed until millions of years later...

A Star is born...
The Universe carried on COOLING, and GRAVITY pulled the hydrogen and helium closer together
WHOOSH
WHOOSH
...causing NUCLEAR REACTIONS
...which created the first STARS (giant balls of burning GAS) ...and so the first GALAXIES were born.
There are about 100 BILLION stars in the MILKY WAY.
There are HUNDREDS of BILLIONS of galaxies in the Universe.
Some galaxies are SPIRALS, some are ELLIPSES, and some are just BLOBS.
The Milky Way, our galaxy, is a very attractive spiral.
I'm a BLOB and proud of it!

It would take 100,000 years to cross the Milky Way if you were travelling at the speed of light...
Nng nngg
which is unlikely - light travels 300,000 km in one second!
Krk krk
Galaxies spin round too. The Earth's bit of the spiral spins round the centre of the Milky Way once every 220 million years.
Galaxies hurtle through space, some faster than others.
More on that later.
We're hoping to see some TERRESTRIALS!
Long before our Sun existed, some of these first stars began to die ...

SUPERNOVAS
When a STAR has burned up all its hydrogen it starts to do this...
WHIZZ
NUCLEAR REACTION
FIZZ
BANG
Small stars will expand to become RED GIANTS.
Heh heh
Not this kind and we've got the colour wrong anyway...
URK
But if it's VERY big, the dying star explodes as a SUPERNOVA... which can burn brighter than all the other stars in its galaxy put together
BANG
BANG
The NUCLEAR REACTIONS and explosions make atoms fuse together to create new, different atoms...
The explosions scatter us throughout the Universe.
Whee!
A billion or so years after the Universe began, the first exploding stars meant that hydrogen and helium atoms at last had some new friends
Hello there!
I'm an oxygen atom.
Lovely weather.
Complicated atoms... like URANIUM... are the results of many supernovas over millions of years.

There are 92 different natural CHEMICAL ELEMENTS on Earth. All of them, except hydrogen and some helium, were made inside stars.
Atoms link together to form MOLECULES and that's how we get WATER...
Ooh... let's cuddle up and get WET!
And molecules combine to make more complicated things like this...
and this...
and this...
And even this...
Gosh!
Around 10^{28} atoms in here (that's 10 with 28 zeros after it!)
The astounding truth is that we are all made from STARS!
IRON atoms in BLOOD
DNA... the building block of life... formed from atoms.
Good grief!
CALCIUM atoms in TEETH
But billions of years before people arrived, another star began to twinkle...

The Sun
Long after the Big Bang, a huge cloud of hydrogen and helium was whizzing through space...
Whooshy WHOOSH
Dust and stuff in here too, made from other STARS.
Suddenly...
WHUMP!!!!
it was squished into a DISC.
Hmm... maybe because of a nearby supernova?
From the huge disc of gases our SUN was formed...
Like other stars, the Sun is a giant ball of burning hydrogen gas... It is the closest star to Earth.
Inside the Sun, NUCLEAR REACTIONS turn 240 tonnes of hydrogen into heat and light EVERY MINUTE
At its core, the temperature is around 15 MILLION° C!
Whew!!
Hmm? hmm?
Why? Why?
The Sun is more than a MILLION MILLION times bigger than the Earth.
Great gas bubbles pop out of the CORONA during SUN STORMS.
BLIP BLOP
The corona extends millions of kilometres out into space from the surface of the Sun. It's nowhere near as bright as the surface, yet it's millions of degrees HOTTER This puzzles scientists.

Hang on, if the Sun's burning all that ENERGY every day, isn't it going to run out of FUEL?
Oh yes!
It's going to EXPAND, become a red giant, and CONSUME the Earth!
chew chew
But not for another 5 BILLION years!
Phew!!
When the Sun formed, there were other bits of dust and metal floating about around it.
Over millions of years, the bits and pieces COLLIDED and were held together by GRAVITY.
WHUMP!!
Biff!
Oof!
CRUNCH
CRASH!!!

And, eventually, there was...

OUR SOLAR SYSTEM
The planets and moons that ORBIT our Sun formed 46 billion years ago.
Hitch-hiking not recommended.
Dwarf planets
Neptune
Uranus
Saturn
Jupiter
Asteroid Belt
Mars
Earth
Venus
Mercury
The Sun
Even though it speeds along, light still takes A DAY to cross our solar system.

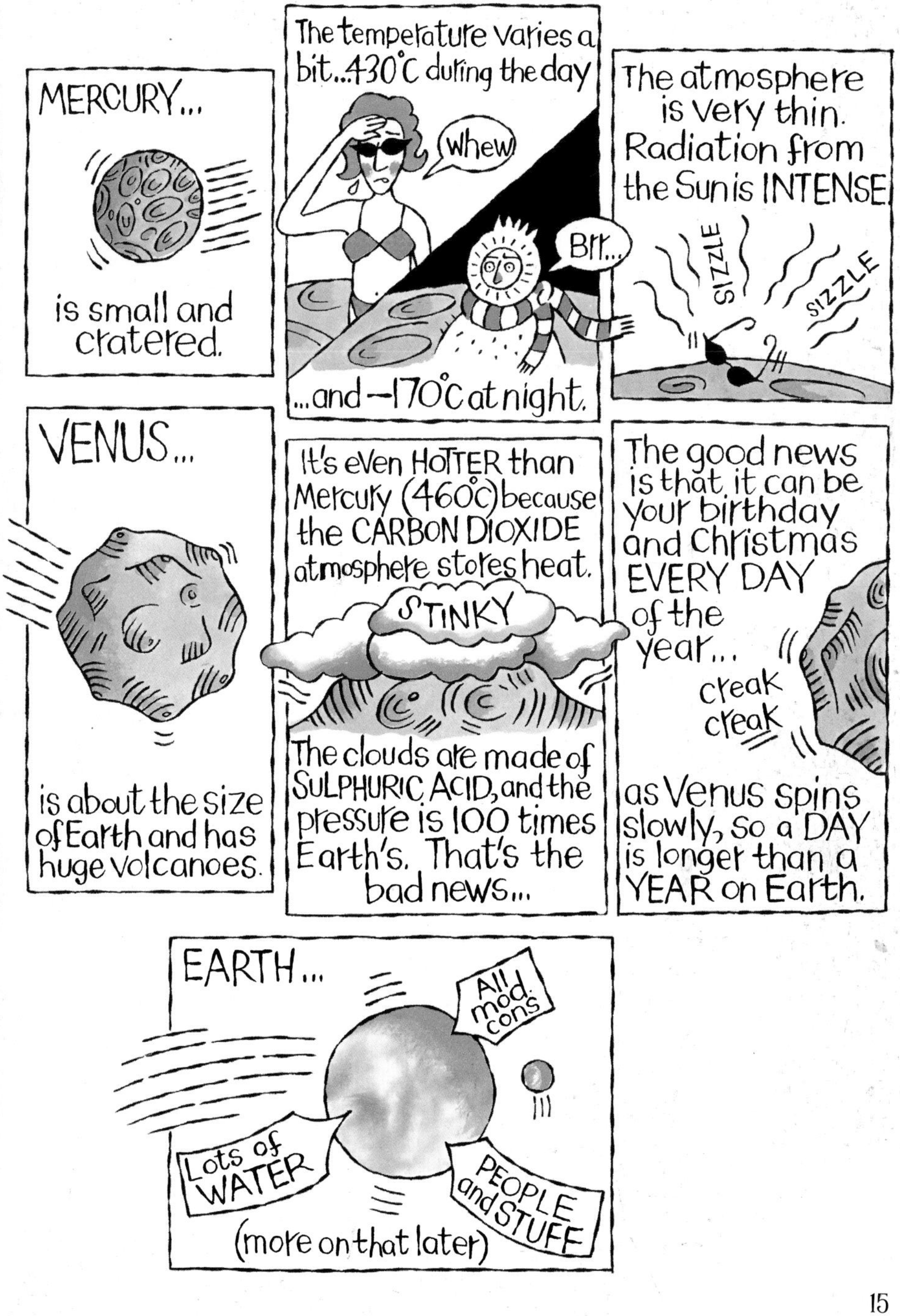
MERCURY...
is small and cratered.
The temperature varies a bit...430°C during the day
Whew
Brr...
...and –170°C at night.
The atmosphere is very thin. Radiation from the Sun is INTENSE.
SIZZLE
SIZZLE
VENUS...
is about the size of Earth and has huge volcanoes.
It's even HOTTER than Mercury (460°C) because the CARBON DIOXIDE atmosphere stores heat.
STINKY
The clouds are made of SULPHURIC ACID, and the pressure is 100 times Earth's. That's the bad news...
The good news is that it can be your birthday and Christmas EVERY DAY of the year...
creak creak
as Venus spins slowly, so a DAY is longer than a YEAR on Earth.
EARTH...
All mod. cons
Lots of WATER
PEOPLE and STUFF
(more on that later)

MARS
CANYONS
Deimos
Phobus
has the highest MOUNTAINS in the solar system.
People thought there might be LIFE on Mars...
Look! There's a canal system...
I hope the MARTIANS are friendly!
If there ever was life, it looked like this...
simple BACTERIA
and died out millions of years ago.
Little do you know, foolish earthlings!
Nng!
ASTEROID BELT
JUPITER...
GREAT RED SPOT
Jupiter's a GAS GIANT–as are Saturn, Uranus and Neptune
is absolutely HUGE... twice as HEAVY as all the other planets put together.
Jupiter is a giant ball of LIQUID and GAS (though there's a core of solid hydrogen).
SQUOOOOSH
An enormous HURRICANE has been raging away on Jupiter for more than 300 years (this is Jupiter's famous Great Red Spot).

SATURN...
RINGS of ICE
lots of MOONS
is also very BIG.
Saturn is another GASSY planet. It's very cold (–176°C) and even windier than Jupiter.
WHOOSH
Brrr!
One of Saturn's moons, TITAN, is bigger than the planet Mercury.
URANUS...
lots of MOONS
Very stinky
is four times the size of Earth, colder than Saturn, and covered in liquid METHANE.
Uranus wasn't discovered until 1780.
Hello! I'm WILLIAM HERSCHEL.
Ooh!
Find out about that on page 50.
One of its moons, PUCK, has three craters called BOGLE, LOB and BUTZ.
NEPTUNE...
raging storms
WHOOSH
WHOOSH
is rather like Uranus but it has 2000 Km/h WINDS.
Neptune wasn't discovered until 1846. It takes so long to orbit the Sun that a year on Neptune is 165 EARTH YEARS.
Read how on page 51.
I'm JOHANN GALLE. I found it!
There used to be a ninth planet called PLUTO, but it's been demoted to a dwarf planet because it's so SMALL.
Sniff sniff

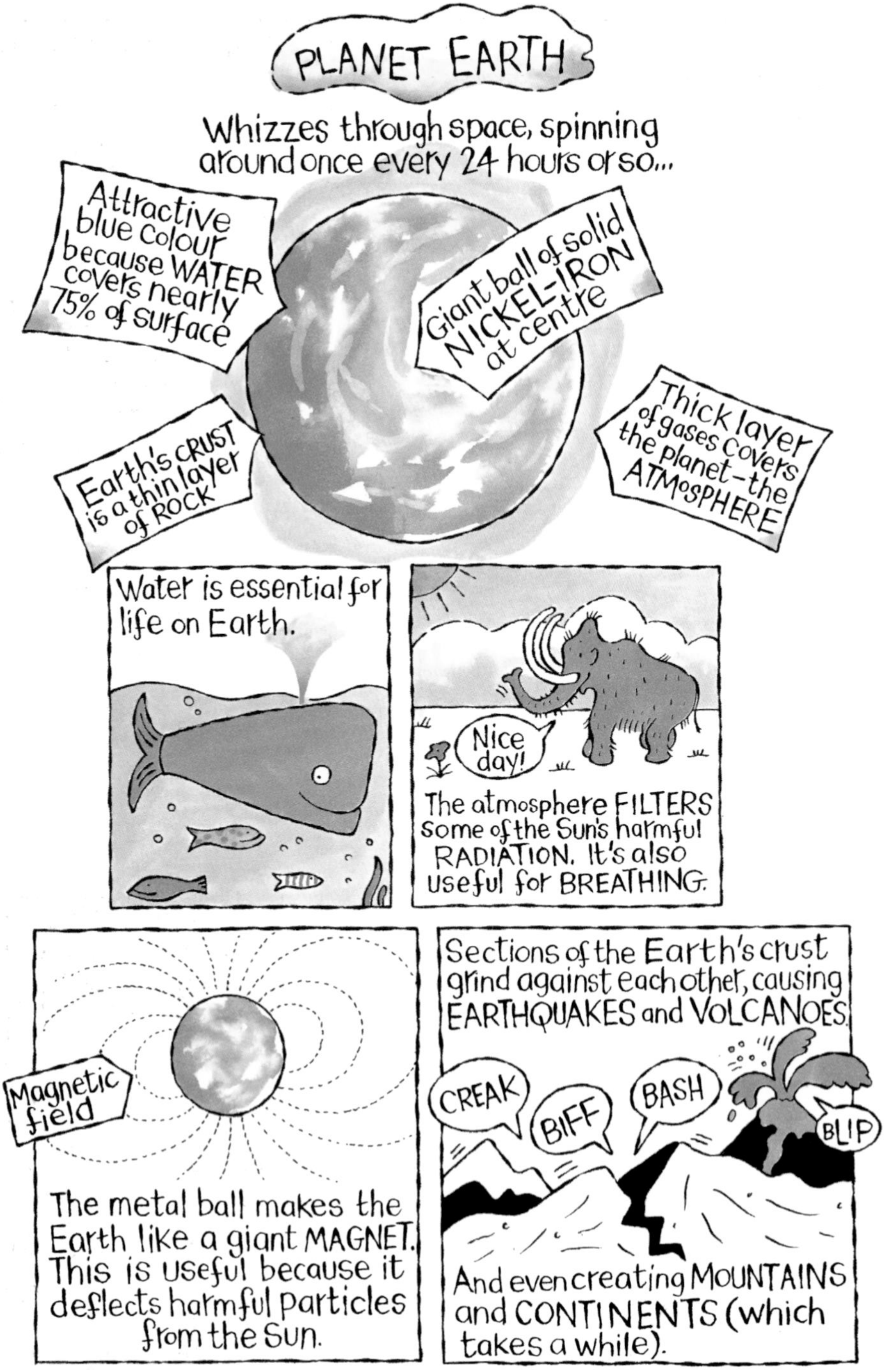
PLANET EARTH
Whizzes through space, spinning around once every 24 hours or so...
Attractive blue colour because WATER covers nearly 75% of surface
Giant ball of solid NICKEL-IRON at centre
Earth's CRUST is a thin layer of ROCK
Thick layer of gases covers the planet – the ATMOSPHERE
Water is essential for life on Earth.
Nice day!
The atmosphere FILTERS some of the Sun's harmful RADIATION. It's also useful for BREATHING.
Magnetic field
The metal ball makes the Earth like a giant MAGNET. This is useful because it deflects harmful particles from the Sun.
Sections of the Earth's crust grind against each other, causing EARTHQUAKES and VOLCANOES.
CREAK
BIFF
BASH
BLIP
And even creating MOUNTAINS and CONTINENTS (which takes a while).

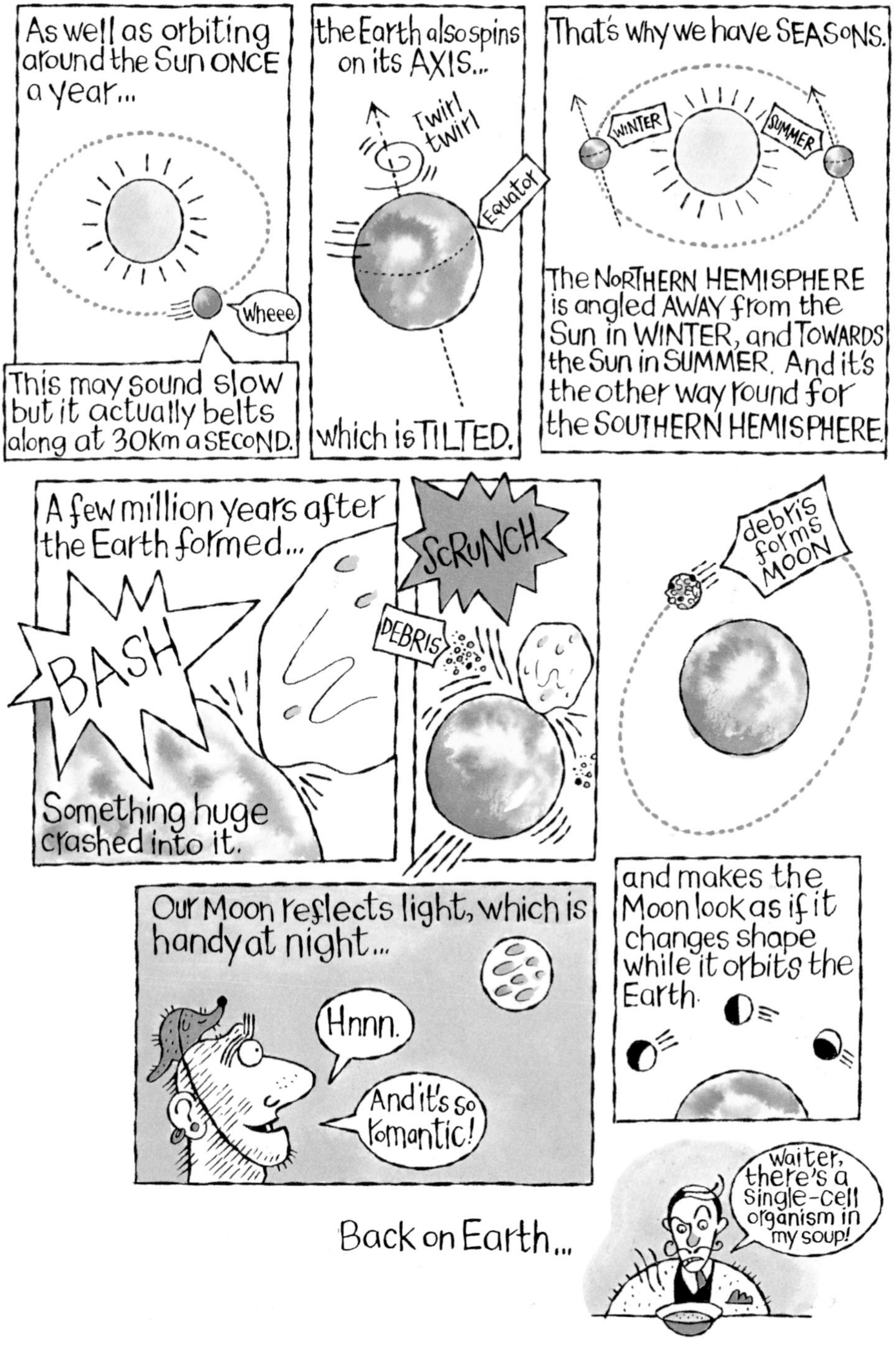
As well as orbiting around the Sun ONCE a year...
Wheee
This may sound slow but it actually belts along at 30km a SECOND.
the Earth also spins on its AXIS...
Twirl twirl
Equator
which is TILTED.
That's why we have SEASONS.
WINTER
SUMMER
The NORTHERN HEMISPHERE is angled AWAY from the Sun in WINTER, and TOWARDS the Sun in SUMMER. And it's the other way round for the SOUTHERN HEMISPHERE.
A few million years after the Earth formed...
BASH
Something huge crashed into it.
SCRUNCH
DEBRIS
debris forms MOON
Our Moon reflects light, which is handy at night...
Hnnn.
And it's so romantic!
and makes the Moon look as if it changes shape while it orbits the Earth.
Back on Earth...
Waiter, there's a single-cell organism in my soup!

life on earth
hisss
blip
blop
hisss!
primordial soup
A few hundred million years later (no one knows how or where) ORGANISMS appeared...
Yoo hoo!
Then...
Later...
Later still...
There was bluey-green ALGAE for about 3 billion years.
Then...
Until...
KK!
Oi!
KKK!
DINOSAURS were around for 175 million years.

Meanwhile, a great CONTINENT had formed.
PANGAEA
one big continent
Gradually...
the continents we know today were created.
Around 65 million years ago (probably)...
an ASTEROID (huge lump of rock) or COMET (huge lump of rock and ice) crashed into Earth.
WHUMP
URK
Now, warm-blooded creatures had a chance.
Heh heh! At last!
Eventually...
Nnng!
People like us first lived around 50,000 years ago (i.e. very recently).

And we were nosier than the dinosaurs...

Prehistoric People Look Up and Get Curious
People started wondering...
Hmm
Scritch scratch
Ooh...
Er...
The Sun gives us light and heat.
We don't like the cold and dark.
Nng nng
Hnn hnn
We certainly don't!
And the Sun and Moon divide time in chunks.
See you at next full Moon then.
Righty-ho.
The changes of the Sun, Moon and stars show us when to plant and harvest.
Yum!

But what are the Sun, Moon and stars really?
Hmm, tricky
... and who controls them eh?
Maybe...
or
or
Yikes!
They must be GODs! We'd better make sure they're happy by PRAYING a lot!
We should do something really BIG to honour them!
Maybe we should slaughter a chicken?!
Oh, honestly!
Some prehistoric people built huge MONUMENTS...
At midsummer Sun rises here
It's a bit draughty but we're working on it...
Cleverly worked out so midwinter Sun sets here
We don't know what STONEHENGE was used for. Maybe it was a TEMPLE or maybe a sort of OBSERVATORY.

People had interesting ideas about what MIGHT be going on UP THERE...

Ancient Thoughts
In the INDIAN HINDU religion...
I'm SURYA the Sun god.
I am VERY powerful
... but the wife's always complaining!
What a scorcher!
Phew!
wheee!
whinny
snort
The GREEK Sun god drove a chariot across the sky.
In SCANDINAVIA...
SKY = SKULL
BRAINS
PLANTS = HAIR
The world's made from a dead FROST GIANT.
Oooh!
The Sun and Moon are sparks from the LAND of FIRE.
Gosh...
Fancy a beer?

In AUSTRALIA...
The stars are the campfires of the sky people.
There certainly are an awful lot of them!
The MAYA worshipped a jaguar-headed god.
I am KINICH AHAU
Nnnnng
He visited the city of Itzamal every day disguised as a macaw.
Yum, lovely!
SQUARK SQUARK
In JAPANESE myth...
blip!
blip
I'm AMATERASU, the Sun goddess.
I was born from the left eye of the supreme being.
Hmmf, that'll teach him!
She hid in a cave after a row with her brother...
Oh, all right then.
But eventually she came out again.
But the Babylonians were the REAL smartypants...

THE ANCIENT BABYLONIANS

The BABYLONIANS were the first to name and number the stars and planets...
We can use our maths
to predict their movements!
scritch scratch
scritch scratch
Gosh, there's another one!
Babylonian clay tablets are the oldest astronomical records in the world.
They believed the stars and planets were ruled by GODS.
The Sun is called SHAMASH
...and that's planet NERGAL – the war god.
Ooh!
Later, the GREEKS and ROMANS used the same system as the Babylonians but replaced the Babylonian gods with their own.
I'm an ancient Roman and the planet Nergal is MARS, our own war god.
I'm a modern person, and now Mars is... er... still Mars.
What goes on up there affects what goes on down here on Earth.
So get praying!
HISS
Babylonian observatories were attached to temples.
The movements of the stars and planets were used to make predictions about people's lives.
Aha! Things are looking very promising for your reign, O king.
Oh, smashing!
Keep up the good work!
We also predicted the future using animals' LIVERS, by the way.

The Babylonians were the first people to come up with the ZODIAC.
The Sun travels through the 12 CONSTELLATIONS of the Zodiac during one year
...which makes it very important.
There wasn't a clear difference between ASTRONOMY and ASTROLOGY in ancient times.
Then...
I am an astrologer AND an astronomer.
My calculations predict the Moon rising in Nergal!
Nng!
Eek!
That's bad luck! Everyone stay indoors!
Now...
Hmm... You're a Pisces, creative and kind, though easily led.
Astrology! Superstitious nonsense!
Pah!
The Babylonians got a few things wrong...
The Earth is FLAT!
Definitely!
Yes, flat!
You see, when it sets in the West, the Sun travels along a canal on a boat round the edge of the world through the night, to rise in the East!
W
EARTH
E
Despite a few mistakes, later civilisations based their astronomy on Babylonian ideas.
We couldn't have done it without you!
Oh, it was nothing really.

They also thought up names for the constellations...

Constellations

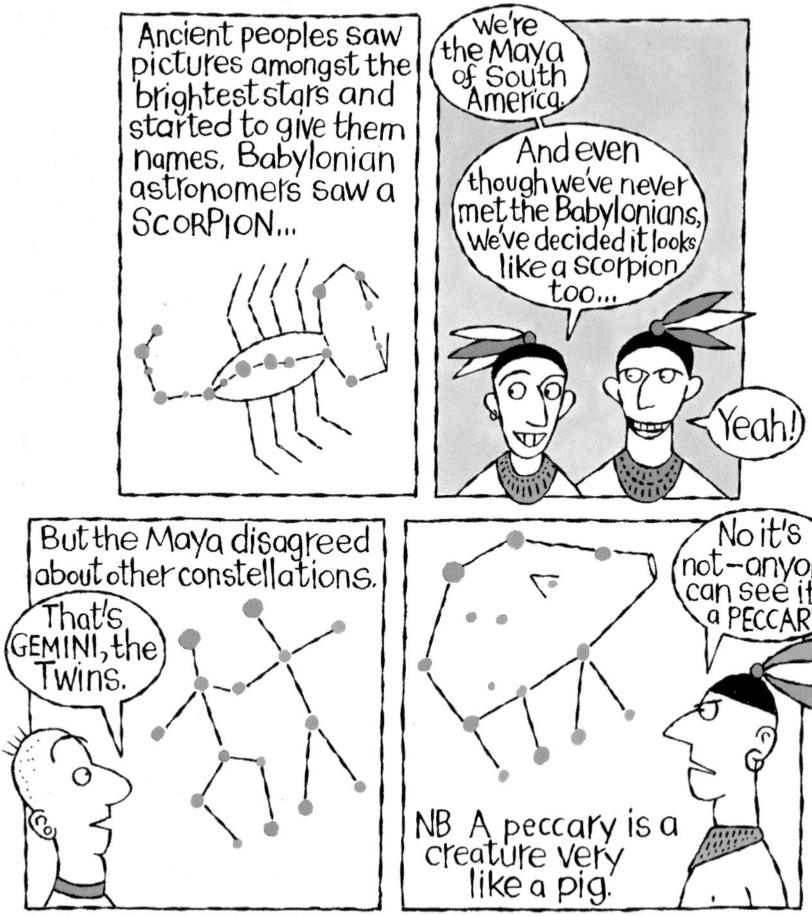

Ancient peoples saw pictures amongst the brightest stars and started to give them names. Babylonian astronomers saw a SCORPION...
We're the Maya of South America.
And even though we've never met the Babylonians, we've decided it looks like a scorpion too...
Yeah!
But the Maya disagreed about other constellations.
That's GEMINI, the Twins.
No it's not – anyone can see it's a PECCARY!
NB A peccary is a creature very like a pig.

What you see in the night sky depends on the time of year and where you are on Earth. And whether or not it's cloudy.

There are some stars I can't see because they're only visible from the Southern hemisphere.
And there are some I can't see. But there are quite a few we can BOTH see.

ORION is one of the easiest constellations to spot in the night sky.
We call it Orion today because that's what the ancient Greeks called it.
Orion was a hunter killed by the gods for being CHEEKY!
Ooh!
Orion looked like a human figure to other ancient peoples too.
But we called it the SHEPHERD of ANU.
In EGYPT, it's SAH, boyfriend of the goddess SOPDET, the brightest star in the sky.
Perhaps surprisingly, lots of different people saw this constellation as a GREAT BEAR.
We did!
So did we!
Us too!
The brightest stars form the PLOUGH or the BIG DIPPER.
Because it looks like THIS!
The SOUTHERN CROSS is easy to spot in the southern hemisphere.
People see it differently...
For MAORIS...
ANCHOR of the Milky Way
In INDONESIA...
STINGRAY
For ABORIGINES...
POSSUM
&
Head of the GREAT EMU in the SKY

Ancient peoples weren't only interested in space by night...

Ancient Chinese Ideas

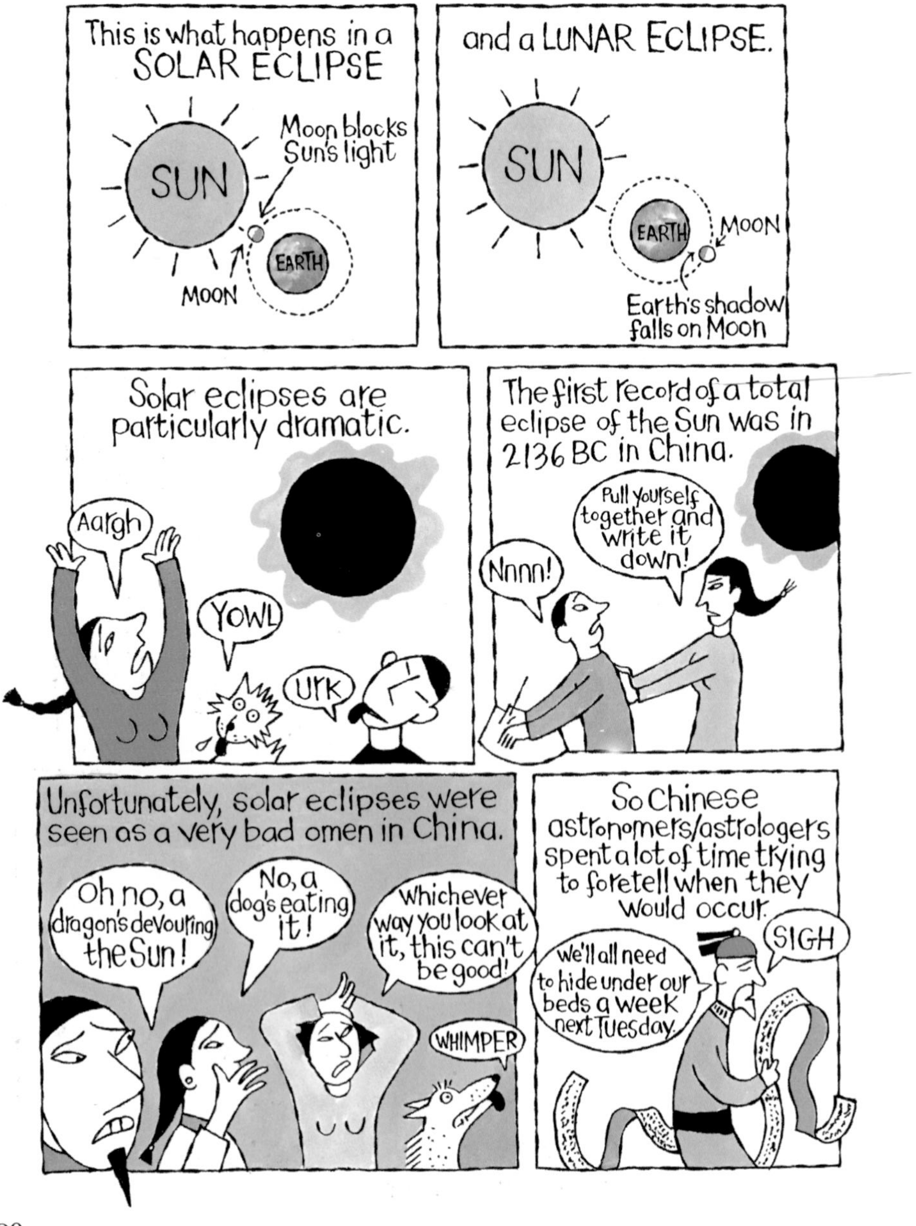

This is what happens in a SOLAR ECLIPSE
SUN
Moon blocks Sun's light
EARTH
MOON
and a LUNAR ECLIPSE.
SUN
EARTH
MOON
Earth's shadow falls on Moon
Solar eclipses are particularly dramatic.
Aargh
YOWL
URK
The first record of a total eclipse of the Sun was in 2136 BC in China.
Pull yourself together and write it down!
Nnnn!
Unfortunately, solar eclipses were seen as a very bad omen in China.
Oh no, a dragon's devouring the Sun!
No, a dog's eating it!
Whichever way you look at it, this can't be good!
WHIMPER
So Chinese astronomers/astrologers spent a lot of time trying to foretell when they would occur.
SIGH
We'll all need to hide under our beds a week next Tuesday.

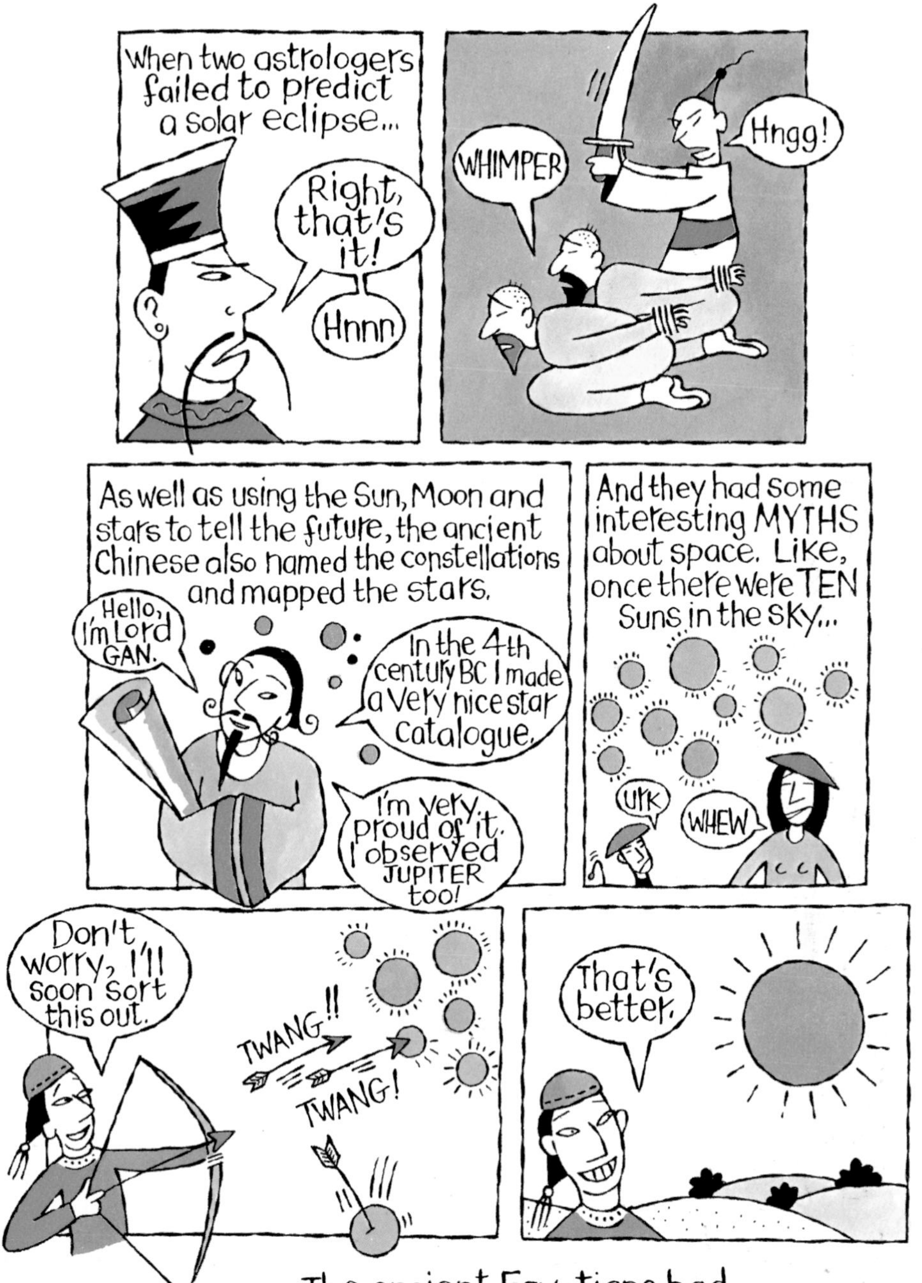
When two astrologers failed to predict a solar eclipse...
Right, that's it!
Hnnn
WHIMPER
Hngg!
As well as using the Sun, Moon and stars to tell the future, the ancient Chinese also named the constellations and mapped the stars.
Hello, I'm Lord GAN.
In the 4th century BC I made a very nice star catalogue.
I'm very proud of it. I observed JUPITER too!
And they had some interesting MYTHS about space. Like, once there were TEN Suns in the sky...
URK
WHEW
Don't worry, I'll soon sort this out.
TWANG!!
TWANG!
That's better.

The ancient Egyptians had some groovy ideas too...

Ancient Egyptian Ideas

Every sunrise, the ancient EGYPTIAN god RE was born.
Gurgle
By midday he was an adult.
By evening, he was old.
Creak
Behave!
Sss!
I want to stop you on your journey!
And at night he travelled through the underworld.
Many other Egyptian gods were seen in the stars.
Look, there's OSIRIS, god of the dead.
So it is!
The MILKY WAY is the goddess NUT giving birth to Re!
I say!

The night sky was divided into groups of STAR GODS travelling in boats.
This is fun!
Ancient Egyptian priests were also astronomers.
We can PREDICT things...
like the annual flooding of the NILE.
The flood was important, which made the priests important too.
The flood is coming!
It happens after the bright star SIRIUS rises before the Sun.
Isn't he clever.
From around 2000 BC, Egyptian astronomers recognised FIVE planets (which we know as Mercury, Venus, Mars, Jupiter and Saturn).
*SBG is bright tonight.
Is that good or bad?
*Sbg was an ancient Egyptian name for Mercury.
Some Egyptian buildings were aligned with the stars.

But the ancient Greeks had some REALLY good ideas...

ANCIENT GREEK THOUGHTS

About 2,500 years ago...

Hello. I'm PYTHAGORUS and...
The Earth is a SPHERE.
Also:
c
a
b
And don't eat beans
Ahem.
My name's ANAXAGORAS
The Sun and stars are fiery stones.
Gosh!
Just call me PLATO. I lived between 428 and 348.
Planets move at a constant speed along circular paths*
*which isn't quite right actually.
I'm his student, ARISTOTLE.
The Sun, Moon and planets revolve round Earth*
*which is completely wrong but an easy mistake.

In the ancient city of ALEXANDRIA...

I'm ARISTARCHUS of Samos and...
actually the Earth revolves round the Sun!
Pah!
Let's ignore him – for a millennium or two!
Aristarchus also worked out how far away the Sun and Moon are.
Hm...

I'm ERATOSTHENES and I worked out the CIRCUMFERENCE of the Earth.
... using sticks and shadows.
Hmm... about 40,000Km...
And he was right!
I mapped the stars and their brightness, and worked out the distance and size of the Moon.
I'm HIPPARCHUS by the way.
PTOLEMY'S theory of an EARTH-CENTRED universe was popular for more than a thousand years.
SUN
EARTH
Neat, isn't it?
A Greek writer, LUCIAN of SAMOSATA, wrote the first ever space travel story.
I feel sick!
In the story, the Moon people are at war with the Sun people. Eventually the travellers return to Earth where they become trapped in a whale.
Grrr
Argh!

Meanwhile, back in the real world...

DARK AGE ASTRONOMERS

In EUROPE, nobody bothered thinking about space much
All that maths and stuff...
Who cares?
Anyone for a rampage?
Learned works of civilised world go up in smoke.
At ALEXANDRIA, the great library was burned down.
In INDIA, BRAHMAGUPTA had some clever thoughts...
The Earth is a moving sphere.
The Moon is illuminated by the Sun.
Hmm
In POLYNESIA, people had become star experts to help them navigate thousands of Kilometres by sea.
Follow that star!
In NORTH AMERICA, the ANASAZI people painted the bright supernova explosion they'd observed in the sky.
Good heavens!
And in CHINA...
We noticed this too!

ISLAMIC scholars were busy translating ancient ideas...
This scroll by Brahmagupta looks interesting.
Hmm...
And this one by Ptolemy too!
Hmm, Earth-centred universe eh?
And writing their own books about space.
I'm al-Khwarizmi and...
I'm good at algebra and algorithms.
Ooh... I'm such a brainbox!
In the 10th century...
I'm al-Sufi.
This is my Book of Fixed Stars.
It includes 'A Little Cloud.'
Little Cloud
The Azophi crater on the Moon is named after al-Sufi.
Al-Sufi's 'cloud' is the ANDROMEDA galaxy: he was the first to spot it.
Then, Islamic astronomers started to find problems with Ptolemy's view of the Universe.
scritch scratch
Hmm
tug tug
Hang on, this can't be right!
Hmm
Does this really make any sense?
Later, a European studying these Islamic astronomers made a PREPOSTEROUS claim...

Copernicus

NICOLAUS COPERNICUS, a Polish astronomer, was about to change space for ever.
Earth
Some planets seem to go backwards in the night sky!
Hmm... I wonder if Ptolemy's system is right?
The Big Book of Islamic Astronomers
Aha! I know!

Copernicus's universe...

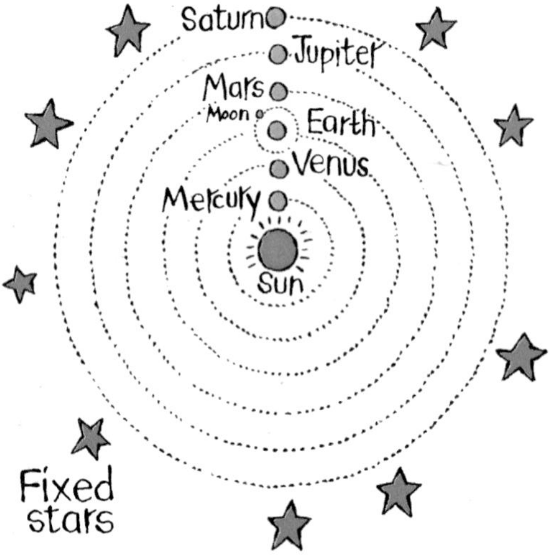

Saturn
Jupiter
Mars
Moon
Earth
Venus
Mercury
Sun
Fixed stars

Copernicus showed a few of his friends and other astronomers...
Here, have a look at this...
Gosh!
My word!
But he didn't publish his work. Maybe he was afraid of what the Church would say...
Of course the Earth is the centre of everything!
Heresy!
We don't hold with this science malarkey!
Nng
Or maybe he was such a perfectionist he was never satisfied.
Hmm... Maybe that just needs a small adjustment...
Eventually, in 1543, he was persuaded by a friend to publish a book showing his new ideas.
Oh for goodness' sake get on with it!
Oh, all right.
New
De Revolutionibus Orbium Coelestium
Buy one get one FREE
But by that time...
URK
In 1616, all books by Copernicus were BANNED. Until 1835.
Read it at your peril!
Lies!
The Devil's work etc, etc.

But Copernicus's calculations couldn't explain the way the planets moved...

Kepler, Brahe (and Moose)

JOHANNES KEPLER was a German mathematician and astronomer.
I do a bit of ASTROLOGY too, just for a laugh.
I'm a Taurus with my moon in Mars, by the way.
I'm the best mathematician!
No, I am!
Take that!
Nng
What's the square root of 658?
TYCHO BRAHE was a Danish nobleman.
...who lost his nose in a duel...
I say!
Smart!
and wore a false gold one.
Brahe liked a party...
You're my besht friend.
HIC
HIC
and so did his pet moose.
He was a brilliant astronomer too.
I discovered a new star in 1572
even though I never used a TELESCOPE
and I'm Imperial Mathematician to the Holy Roman Emperor!
Brahe invited Kepler to work as his assistant, though they didn't get on too well...
Posh drunken fool.
Boring little whippersnapper.
After just 18 months...
Heh heh
Urk
Finally I can get my hands on Brahe's lovely astronomical data!

Kepler worked out what was wrong with Copernicus's universe...
Got it!
The planets travel round an ELLIPSE, not a circle, with the Sun to one side!
Planets travel faster when closest to the Sun!
And there's a mathematical rule about how long it takes a planet to orbit the Sun.
Phew!
Hmm... I wonder what the force is that keeps planets in their orbits?
Scritch Scratch

Kepler also wrote a story about space...

Moon craters carved out by moon people
Moon mountains
Moon seas

But being a scientific genius in those days was not without problems...

Galileo

GALILEO GALILEI was an Italian astronomer, mathematician and philosopher.
And physicist actually.
Among other things, he improved the design of the newly invented TELESCOPE*
Oooh!
*His design and lenses meant he could MAGNIFY by 30 times.
And discovered the moons of JUPITER.
Golly...
Four of them orbiting Jupiter. It's a bit like the planets going round the Sun.
(We now know Jupiter has loads of moons... about 60... but we do have better telescopes.)
Galileo also discovered that the planet VENUS has phases...
Caused by the Sun shining on it as Venus orbits.
This helps prove that the Sun's at the centre, not the Earth.
And that SATURN has something a bit STRANGE going on...
Hmm... Saturn appears to have EARS!
Unfortunately...
The Earth goes round the Sun and these observations seem to... um... prove it!
Gnash!
Nnng!
In 1635, Galileo was condemned by the church and sentenced to house arrest. Seven years later...
URK

Huygens

Meanwhile, in Holland, CHRISTIAAN HUYGENS agreed with Galileo. Like him he was good at everything.
Luckily I managed to avoid going to prison though!
Huygens described Martian geography.
And I worked out how long it takes Mars to spin on its axis.
Mars
mountains
Wheee!
He worked out that Saturn's 'ears' were actually RINGS
And he also discovered Saturn's largest moon.
TITAN
SATURN
In my spare time I invented the PENDULUM CLOCK!
Tick tock!
Huygens also wondered about travelling to space in ships...
Morning!
And he imagined other planets populated by inhabitants a bit like us.
???
But what about the invention that helped Galileo and Huygens to see things clearly?

Telescopes

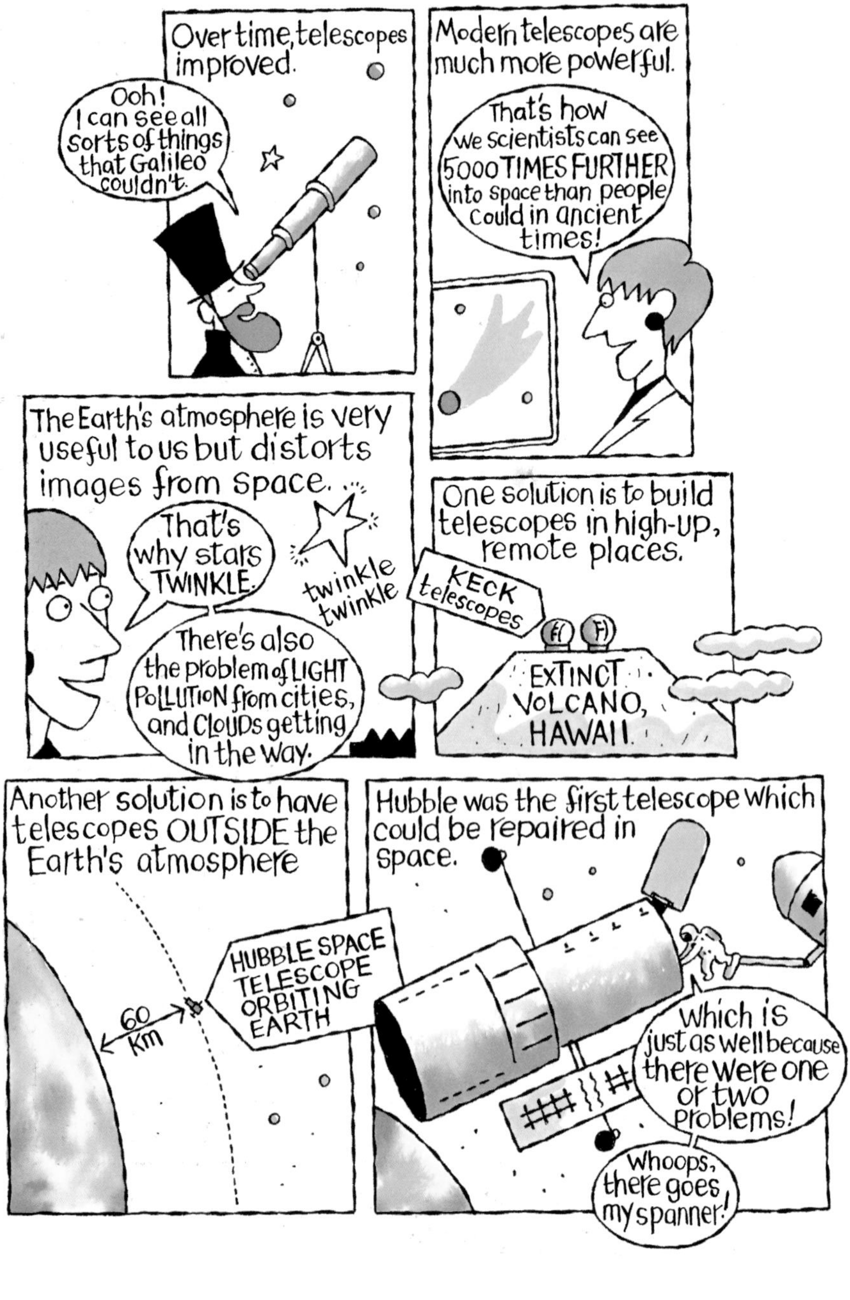
Over time, telescopes improved.
Ooh! I can see all sorts of things that Galileo couldn't.
Modern telescopes are much more powerful.
That's how we scientists can see 5000 TIMES FURTHER into space than people could in ancient times!
The Earth's atmosphere is very useful to us but distorts images from space.
That's why stars TWINKLE.
twinkle twinkle
There's also the problem of LIGHT POLLUTION from cities, and CLOUDS getting in the way.
One solution is to build telescopes in high-up, remote places.
KECK telescopes
EXTINCT VOLCANO, HAWAII
Another solution is to have telescopes OUTSIDE the Earth's atmosphere
60 Km
HUBBLE SPACE TELESCOPE ORBITING EARTH
Hubble was the first telescope which could be repaired in space.
Which is just as well because there were one or two problems!
Whoops, there goes my spanner!

Hubble has taken the most detailed pictures of the most distant objects in the Universe...

Pillars of Creation in EAGLE NEBULA
SOMBRERO GALAXY
Cosmic Pearl round an exploding star
CAT'S EYE NEBULA
Remains of supernova
KINDBERG GALAXY (OK, I made that up. It's a tea stain.)

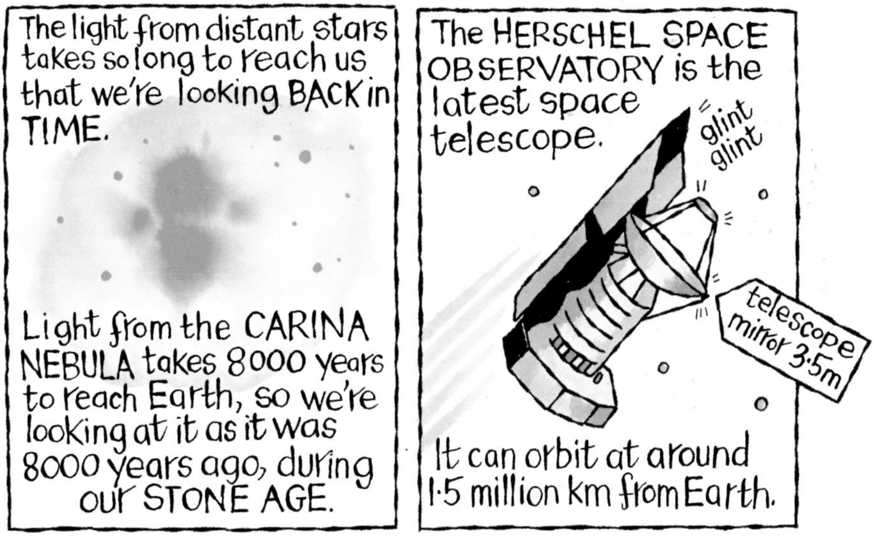

The light from distant stars takes so long to reach us that we're looking BACK in TIME.
Light from the CARINA NEBULA takes 8000 years to reach Earth, so we're looking at it as it was 8000 years ago, during our STONE AGE.
The HERSCHEL SPACE OBSERVATORY is the latest space telescope.
glint glint
telescope mirror 3·5m
It can orbit at around 1·5 million km from Earth.

Telescopes are useful, but it helps if you're a bit of a boffin too...

NEWTON

Scientific genius ISAAC NEWTON worked out the mysterious force that had puzzled Kepler...
Hmmm... The Moon is in orbit around the Earth. What stops it whizzing off into space?
Moon
Earth
There must be a force acting between them!
I'll call it GRAVITY!
Ouch!!
Aha!
Could gravity have something to do with why things drop downwards here on Earth?
munch munch
The more massive the objects, the STRONGER the pull between them...
The further away the massive objects are
the WEAKER the force of gravity...
Gosh!
Have you heard the latest?
$Fg=G\frac{m_1m_2}{r^2}$!
Cheeky!!

Gravity explains why planets move more slowly the further away from the Sun they are.
slower here
faster here
Whole GALAXIES are held together by the force of gravity.
Newton's laws were the first that could apply on Earth and in space too.
The same force that makes an apple fall makes the Moon go round the Earth
...and the Earth go round the Sun.
Gravity also explains the TIDES of the SEA.
EARTH
MOON
In his spare time, Newton also invented CALCULUS...
dy/dt = dy/du · du/dt
etc.
etc.
Er... I'm LEIBNIZ, and so did I, actually!
Newton worked out that white light was made up of the COLOUR SPECTRUM
Amazing!
...and tried to make GOLD out of ordinary metal.
Umm, yes. Bit embarrassing, that...

And Newton had some clever chums...

COMETS!
EDMOND HALLEY was a mate of Newton's.
Yes, in fact I persuaded him to publish his work - he'd kept quiet about it for years!
Thanks, Ed!
He was also an astronomer.
I wrote a book about the southern stars.
In his spare time he made one of the first DIVING BELLS.
But he was most famous for...
COMETS are huge space snowballs made of ice, rock and metal.
As a comet travels closer to the Sun, it trails ice and dust behind it.
Comets orbit around the Sun in slightly WONKY paths.
Woe! Woe!
I'm the ancient Greek ARISTOTLE.
Comets cause STRONG WINDS and DROUGHT!
(they don't)
Comets were seen as a sign of DISASTER (which isn't true either - unless you're a DINOSAUR...)
urk

Halley used Newton's theories to work out that a particular comet returned close to the Earth at regular intervals.
Oh no!
It appeared just before the BATTLE of HASTINGS in 1066.
Halley spotted it in 1682...
Hmm... it has the same orbit as one that was last seen in 1607... it's the same one!
He didn't live to see it return as he'd predicted it would in 1758, by which time it had a name.
There goes Halley's Comet!
When Halley's Comet passed by in 1910, comet-protecting UMBRELLAS and anti-comet PILLS went on sale.
I say!
Some special comets...
Comet DONATI, seen in 1858, had 2 tails.
SHOEMAKER-LEVY 9 broke into bits and crashed into JUPITER in 1994.
HALE-BOPP, first seen in 1995, was especially big and bright.
Comet HYAKUTAKE had the longest tail ever – 570 million km (measured in 2000).
Comet-spotting became popular in the 1700s. Astronomer CAROLINE HERSCHEL discovered EIGHT of them.
There's another one!
One of them was named after her.
35P/HERSCHEL-RIGOLLET

But Caroline wasn't as famous as her brother...

New Planets

WILLIAM HERSCHEL was a musician...
BOOMPA BOOMPA
and an astronomer in his spare time.
And he made telescopes, too...
It's a bit complicated, involves moulds using HORSE MANURE.
Pooh!
In 1781, with the help of his sister, the comet-hunter...
Ooh... I've discovered a new comet!
Another one?
YAWN
Hang on! It's not a comet, it's a new PLANET!
Yippee!
The other planets known about at this time (Mercury, Venus, Mars, Jupiter and Saturn) could all be seen with the naked eye.
After some debate, the new planet was called URANUS.
Uranus was the grandfather of Jupiter in classical mythology.
But I still prefer ROGER!

Another NEW PLANET was discovered in 1846.
We're scientists and...
we knew it must have been there...
Because its gravity was affecting Uranus.
We worked it out using Newton's gravity laws and lots of maths.
Phew
I'm JOHANN GALLE.
I was the one who actually found it in the end.
It's called NEPTUNE.
Hurrah!
I'm CLYDE TOMBAUGH.
In 1930, I discovered another planet...
PLUTO!
But since 2006 it doesn't count as a planet any more.
Boo.

But as scientists delved further into space, our imaginations entered orbit as well...

SPACE STORIES
Back in 1668, MARGARET CAVENDISH wrote The Blazing World about a planet you can reach from the Arctic...
With some strange inhabitants,
Greetings, Parrot Man.
Squark!
Sss!
In a 1752 story by VOLTAIRE, a 120,000 ft tall alien called MICROMEGAS...
travels to Earth on passing comets.
Hnn
In the space stories JULES VERNE wrote in the 1800s, three men are fired to the Moon by a cannon called Columbiad.
They orbit the Moon and make it back to Earth...
Whey-hey!
without meeting any aliens (not so different from what happened in 1968).

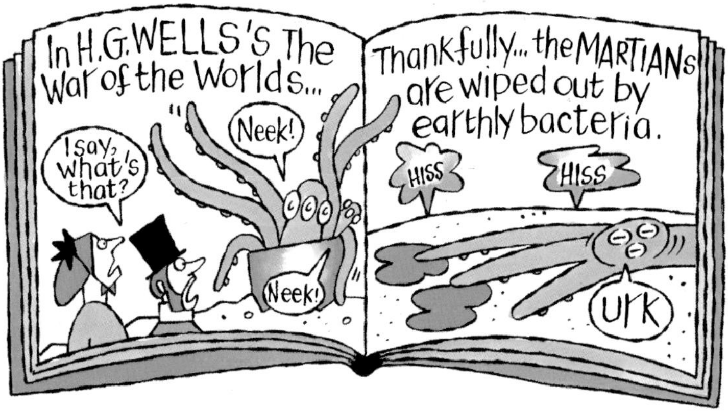
In H.G.WELLS'S The War of the Worlds...
I say, what's that?
Neek!
Neek!
Thankfully... the MARTIANs are wiped out by earthly bacteria.
HISS
HISS
URK

There have been hundreds of SPACE MOVIES...
Not many of them feature friendly aliens...

Hnnn...

I'm one of them though!

And plenty of TV series too...

Beam me up, Scottie!

At the start of the 20th century
in a Swiss patents office...

EINSTEIN

ALBERT EINSTEIN worked full-time in a patents office in Berne.
I help evaluate new INVENTIONS.
Hmm... Nice.
DING
PATENT N
I couldn't get a job teaching science.
In his spare time, he unlocked the secrets of the Universe.
There's a huge amount of ENERGY locked up inside MATTER.
MASS is a form of energy.
Of course... E=mc²!
E=energy
m=mass
c=speed of light
Nothing can travel faster than the SPEED OF LIGHT.
The closer something gets to the speed of light, the greater its mass.
If PING-PONG balls could travel very fast...
And speeds approaching the speed of light can even affect the PASSAGE OF TIME!
Whoosh!!
A spacecraft travels unbelievably fast for 2 years...
but back on Earth, 5 years have passed.
It's all RELATIVE!
This has been proved using accurate clocks in very fast jet planes (only with fractions of seconds, not years).

Sorry, Newton, but your view of space and time isn't right!
???
Gravity is the curvature of the SPACE-TIME CONTINUUM.
GULP
Space-time is just our 3-dimensional world plus the 4th dimension of time, by the way...
I wish he'd just shut up and give me my dinner!
Space curves round massive objects like the Sun.
All the experiments done since Einstein's time prove his theories to be correct.
But I can't make my theories agree with theories about ATOMS.
Zzz
Einstein spent years trying to come up with a theory of EVERYTHING. He didn't manage it.
Er...
Bother.
No one else has either
... but we're still trying!
Meanwhile...

SPEEDING GALAXIES

The biggest TELESCOPE in the world was built on top of MOUNT WILSON in California.
I'm MILTON HUMASON.
Hmm, this looks interesting.
Can I have a go?
Humason got a job as a cleaner at Mount Wilson.
But it turned out he was a brilliant astronomer.
What an amazing supernova!
He's a natural!
Hello there!
Scientist EDWIN HUBBLE came to work at Mount Wilson. Together, they made some amazing discoveries.
A few years before...
I'm VESTO MELVIN SLIPHER.
I observed other GALAXIES that seemed to be moving away from us.
And I'm HENRIETTA LEAVITT. I discovered interesting things about the brightness of STARS.
Thanks to them and other astronomers
...We worked out the distances of other galaxies
...and how fast they're moving.
WHOOSH!

We also discovered that some galaxies are going so FAST they are approaching the SPEED of LIGHT
and the FURTHER away galaxies are, the FASTER they are moving.
... It's HUBBLE's LAW!
ZOOOM!!
Neat, eh?
Using Hubble's Law, the distances to other galaxies could now be measured.
Gosh, they ARE a long way away!
Ooh!
People began to realise the astonishing size of the Universe for the first time.
1 LIGHT YEAR=
EARTH
220 million times round the Earth.
All these other galaxies are MILLIONS of light years away from our galaxy.
The furthest galaxies we can see today are BILLIONS of light years away.
Lemaître here again.
You met me on page 4.
My Big Bang theory was based on Hubble and Humason's work.
Right, I'm off.

Meanwhile, in a galaxy far, far away...

OTHER SOLAR SYSTEMS

Hubble and Humason had revealed the true vastness of the Universe.

But nobody knows much about planets in other solar systems within our own galaxy... let alone solar systems in other galaxies.
Holdonabit, we're only just getting to know the ones in our own solar system.
The first planets outside our own solar system weren't discovered until 1992.
Hello, I'm ALEX WOLSZCZAN.
I found them!
300 or so planets have been proved to exist so far.
But within the visible Universe there are thought to be about 100 thousand million million million planets!

So it's a bit unlikely that planet Earth is the only one in the whole Universe to support life.
GNK! We've got life!
and US!

For all we know...

We are the BLUNGE WORMS of Zorg...
Anyone for a slime?
ooze ooze
We evolved to look like earthly paperclips.
What are the chances of that?

Do our lives have meaning?
Or is life simply absurd?
Nnn

And if we don't know what they look like, how can we be sure they haven't arrived ALREADY...

CLOSE ENCOUNTERS
There have been thousands of reports of UFOs.
That's an UNIDENTIFIED FLYING OBJECT.
YIKES!
LONELY HILL
Some of them remain a MYSTERY, and some people think they are the aircraft of ALIEN BEINGS.
Yoo hoo, Earthling!
We mean you no harm.
Heh heh
The most famous UFO incident happened in New Mexico.
Nothing... unusual... here... at... all...
We recovered a weather balloon near Roswell.
Hnn
It's a government cover-up!
They really recovered a crashed alien spacecraft
...and the dead bodies of real aliens!
PRESS
Urk
Since then, there have been many reports of differently shaped UFOs, like this...
or this...

And SIGHTINGS of aliens...
SALE NOW ON
Nngy nnnng
Take me to your bargains!
shuffle shuffle
and even ABDUCTIONS by aliens.
zinger zinger
I say!
And how do you explain crop circles, eh?
caw caw
The marks of alien spacecraft landing and taking off.
The truth is out there.
Actually it was us, using planks, wire and rope.
No it wasn't. It was an alien spacecraft.
sigh

But the only way to find out what's really out there is to go and check...

SPACE RACE

To get out of Earth's atmosphere and into space, you need a rocket...

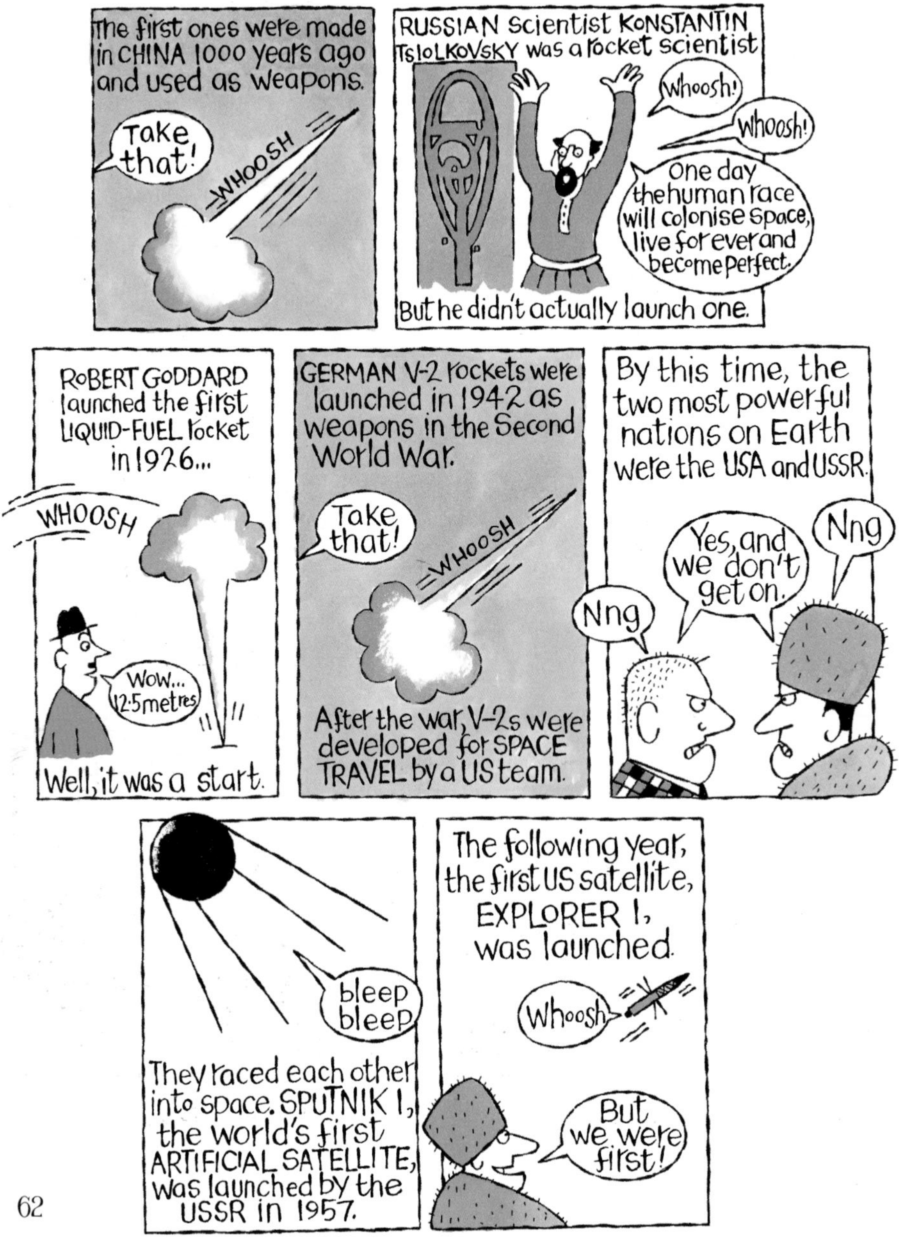
The first ones were made in CHINA 1000 years ago and used as weapons.
Take that!
WHOOSH
RUSSIAN scientist KONSTANTIN TSIOLKOVSKY was a rocket scientist
Whoosh!
Whoosh!
One day the human race will colonise space, live for ever and become perfect.
But he didn't actually launch one.
ROBERT GODDARD launched the first LIQUID-FUEL rocket in 1926...
WHOOSH
Wow... 12.5 metres
Well, it was a start.
GERMAN V-2 rockets were launched in 1942 as weapons in the Second World War.
Take that!
WHOOSH
After the war, V-2s were developed for SPACE TRAVEL by a US team.
By this time, the two most powerful nations on Earth were the USA and USSR.
Nng
Yes, and we don't get on.
Nng
bleep bleep
They raced each other into space. SPUTNIK 1, the world's first ARTIFICIAL SATELLITE, was launched by the USSR in 1957.
The following year, the first US satellite, EXPLORER 1, was launched.
Whoosh
But we were first!

The SOVIETS launched the first spacecraft to leave Earth's gravity...
It was called LUNA 1.
and the first one to land on the Moon.
So put that in your pipe and smoke it, American capitalists!
Plop
The US formed space agency NASA and started spending some serious cash.
I'm the US President!
Right, we're not having this.
We're going to be first to send a person into space!
Come on, get on with it!
But the Russians beat them to it*...
American twerps!
CCCP
*More on this later.
...only by a MONTH, though.
Grrr! That makes it even more annoying!
The Space Race went on for years. Sometimes the US was ahead...
Yeah, like now, Russian losers!
More on this later too...
And sometimes the USSR...
Look at our beautiful space station and weep!
But going back to the start of the race...

ANIMALS IN SPACE
Everyone was keen to get into space.
We can't wait!
But hang on a minute...
we don't know the effects of weightlessness.
How do we know people won't... EXPLODE or Something?
Did she say 'explode'?
GULP
Er... I'm feeling a bit less keen!
So the first living things weren't PEOPLE at all...
GULP
they were fruit flies.
Bzzz!
Whooshy
Since then many more animals have been sent beyond Earth's atmosphere - mostly monkeys, dogs and mice.
Nnng
Urrr
Squeeak
In 1957, LAIKA the dog was the first animal to orbit the Earth.
Urk
Laika didn't make it back to Earth.
STRELKA and BELKA were the first animals to go into orbit and come back alive.
Phew

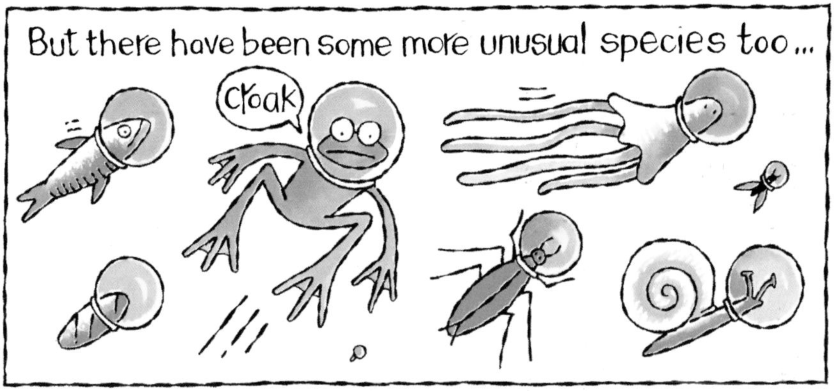

But there have been some more unusual species too...
Croak

Wheee
ARABELLA and ANITA spun the first webs in space.

Bees built a hive in space.
BUZZ
BUZZ
BUZZ

Tortoises hold the record for the longest space flight...
90 long days!

Animals have even been born in space.
cheep cheep

In 1961, the first PERSON went into space...

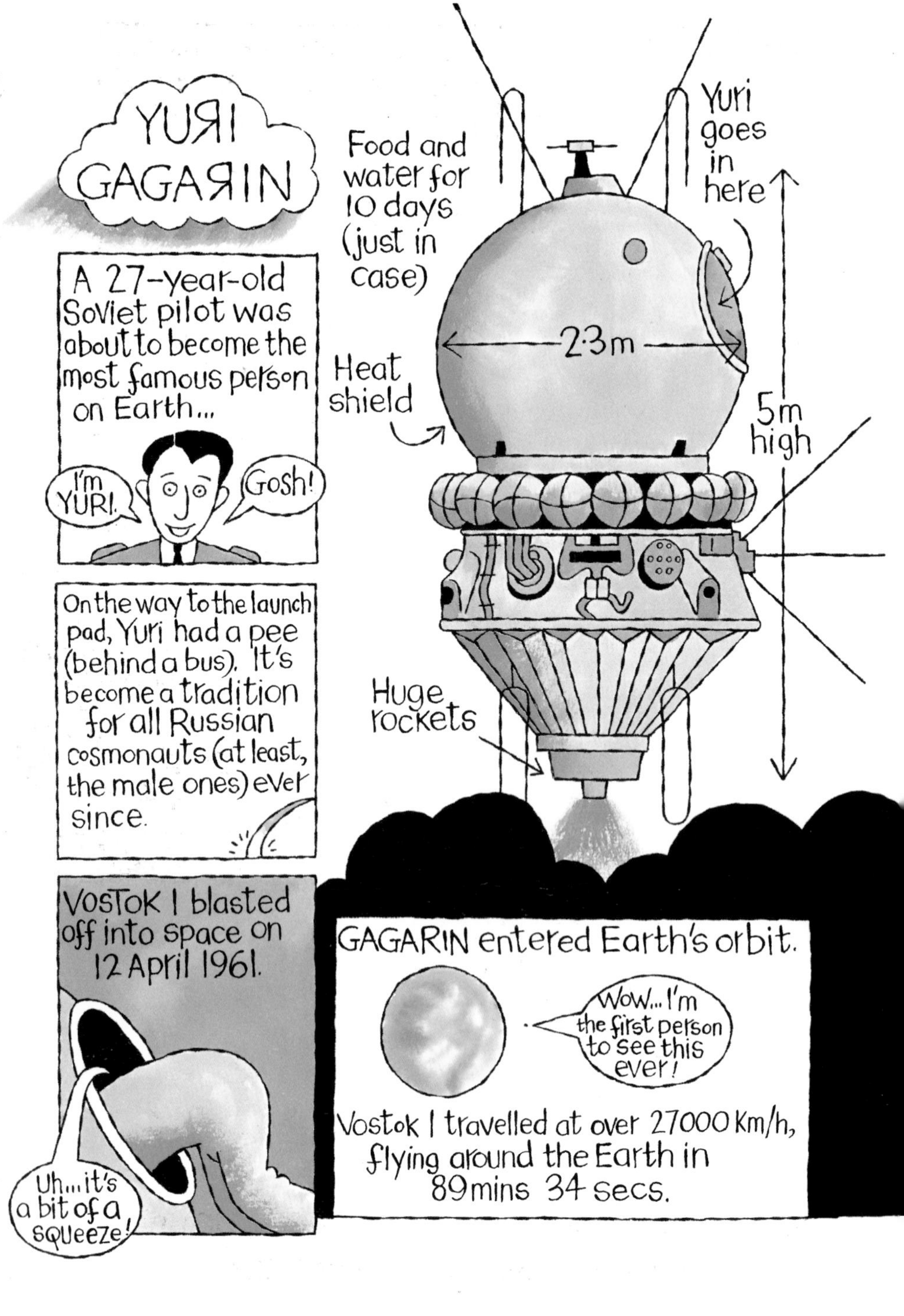

YURI GAGARIN
A 27-year-old Soviet pilot was about to become the most famous person on Earth...
I'm YURI.
Gosh!
On the way to the launch pad, Yuri had a pee (behind a bus). It's become a tradition for all Russian cosmonauts (at least, the male ones) ever since.
VOSTOK I blasted off into space on 12 April 1961.
Uh... it's a bit of a squeeze!
Food and water for 10 days (just in case)
Yuri goes in here
2·3m
Heat shield
5m high
Huge rockets
GAGARIN entered Earth's orbit.
Wow... I'm the first person to see this ever!
Vostok I travelled at over 27000 Km/h, flying around the Earth in 89 mins 34 secs.

Gagarin didn't stay in the spacecraft for landing.
SPLAT!!
...which was just as well.
He ejected at 6100m and parachuted into a field.
Er... hello there!
Nnn
Yuri Gagarin was given the official title of HERO of the SOVIET UNION.
I say!
He paraded round Red Square for six hours.
HURRAR!
HURRAR!
He went on a world tour and did even more parading...
He might be a Communist but what a hero!
SWOON SWOON
And so handsome!
Sadly, Gagarin died in a plane crash in 1968. But he lives on in space: on the far side of the Moon is the GAGARIN CRATER.

The Americans were more determined than ever to win the next leg of the space race...

MOON LANDINGS

I'm the US President, John F. Kennedy.
I want people on the Moon within the next ten years.
No more hanging about being beaten by the Soviets!
Come on, get on with it!
We're ready! And it's still only 1969!
APOLLO 11 blasted off to the Moon on 20 July 1969.
The CREW
I'm Neil.
I'm Michael.
I'm BUZZ.
The command module COLUMBIA was controlled by MICHAEL COLLINS, who didn't land on the Moon.
Bother!
Astronauts landed in lunar module EAGLE.
This is one small step for man, one giant leap for mankind.
I've been practising that for weeks!
NEIL ARMSTRONG was the FIRST PERSON to walk on the Moon.

GRAVITY isn't as strong on the Moon as it is on Earth...
Wheee!
BUZZ ALDRIN was the second Moonwalker in the crew.
The astronauts took samples of lunar rock and dust, made notes and took photographs.
The American flag was planted on the Moon – it had to have a telescopic arm to make it fly without any wind.
Woof!
The landing was broadcast on TV – 500 million people watched.
There were 5 more Apollo missions and 10 more American astronauts walked on the Moon.

And because space was a brand new destination, people were desperate to do things FIRST...

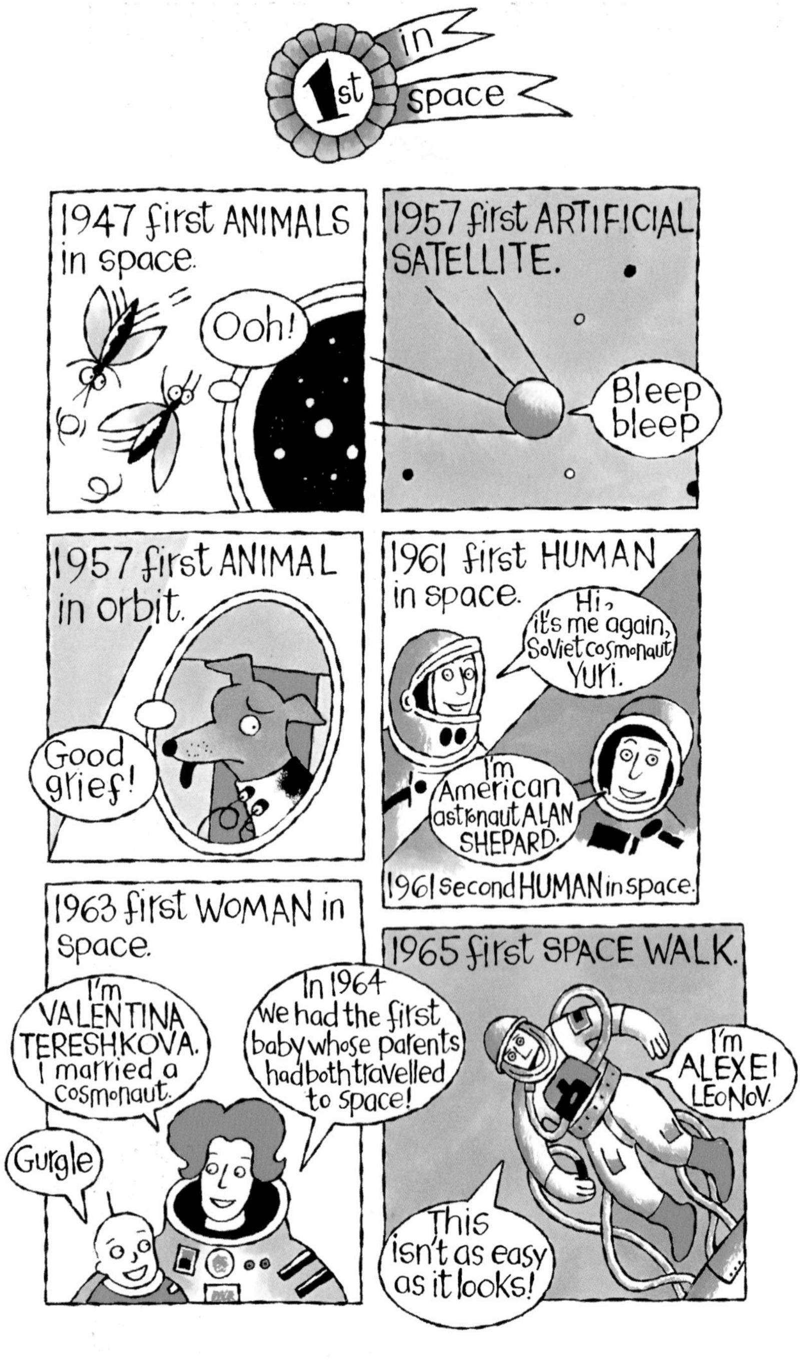
1st in space
1947 first ANIMALS in space.
Ooh!
1957 first ARTIFICIAL SATELLITE.
Bleep bleep
1957 first ANIMAL in orbit.
Good grief!
1961 first HUMAN in space.
Hi, it's me again, Soviet cosmonaut YURI.
I'm American astronaut ALAN SHEPARD.
1961 second HUMAN in space.
1963 first WOMAN in space.
I'm VALENTINA TERESHKOVA. I married a cosmonaut.
In 1964 we had the first baby whose parents had both travelled to space!
Gurgle
1965 first SPACE WALK.
I'm ALEXEI LEONOV.
This isn't as easy as it looks!

1969 first HUMAN on the Moon.
It's NEIL again.
Erm...
It's a big leap for man... a big step for humans... oh bother!
1971 first SPACE STATION.
SALYUT 1
1972 first SPACECRAFT to pass through ASTEROID BELT.
PIONEER 10
BIFF
CLANG
1975 first internationally crewed SPACE STATION.
Howdy!
Привет*
Inside APOLLO-SOYUZ (US/SOVIET)
*Russian for 'Hi'.
1981 first REUSABLE spacecraft, the space SHUTTLE.
That was fun... let's do it again!
1983 first spacecraft to LEAVE our SOLAR SYSTEM.
PIONEER 10 (again)
1990 first space TELESCOPE.
HUBBLE
2001 first SPACE TOURIST.
I'm DENNIS TITO.
Erm... better send a postcard!

Meanwhile, amazing discoveries were still being made...

BLACK HOLES, QUASARS & PULSARS

Back in 1783...
Ahem
Hello, I'm the REVEREND JOHN MICHELL.
The more MASSIVE an object, the FASTER you have to go to escape from its gravity.
So if something's really massive – 500 times bigger than the SUN but just as dense, say...
Surely even LIGHT couldn't go fast enough to escape.
That's plain weird!
Eh?
Let's ignore him!
Until the 20th century.
More recently...
If a really massive star collapses the gravity is so strong that nothing can move fast enough to get out – not even LIGHT.
Great Scott! Michell was right all along!
Modern scientists think...
BLACK HOLES aren't very big...
There's probably a huge black hole at the centre of our GALAXY!
At the centre is a SINGULARITY – INFINITELY dense.
Oooh
urk

We've also discovered QUASARs.
They're extremely powerful and very far away.
They shine brighter than the galaxies that surround them.
We think they surround enormous black holes.
Listen to this!
blip blip blip
It's too regular to be natural!
It must be an ALIEN broadcast!
Like, WOW!
Awesome.
Actually it's not aliens.
It's dense stars called NEUTRON STARS.
A cubic centimetre of a neutron star would weigh a BILLION TONNES.
Heavy!
blip blip
Foolish Earthlings!
Neutron stars called PULSARS spin around, beaming radio waves out into space...
Like powerful space searchlights.

Meanwhile, we sent animals... we sent people...
What could we send into space now?

SPACE PROBES

Sending PEOPLE into space is an awful lot of hassle.
You're telling ME!
SPACE PROBES are less bother. They don't get homesick and it doesn't matter if they're destroyed once they've finished their mission.
Tzzzt!
Tzzz
The first ones were sent to the Moon...
beepa beepa
CCCP
This side is never seen from Earth
LUNA 3 gave us the first pictures of the far side of the Moon.
and Venus.
CCCP
Some space probes fly past planets and send images back to Earth.
Dear Earth, Having a lovely time in Space. Wish you were here. Mariner 9 x
Oooh, look at that!
The Solar and Heliospheric Observatory (SOHO) has been observing the Sun since 1996.

MARS EXPLORATION ROVERS, Spirit and Opportunity, landed on Mars in 2004.
beepa beepa
and they're still sending us information.
PHOENIX is the most recent visitor to Mars.
Some space probes leave our Solar System and sail away into distant space.
Norshy!
Hang on, what's that?
PIONEER 10 and 11 began their long journey to JUPITER in the early seventies. They stopped transmitting to Earth but they're still out there somewhere.
VOYAGER 1 has travelled further from Earth than any other object made by humans.
16 billion Km from the Sun
still transmitting to Earth
beepa beepa
Pioneer and Voyager carry MESSAGES in case they're found by ALIENS.
Gold-plated to protect against space dust
Greetings in 56 languages, 100 photos, binary code
In 1974, a radio message with information about humans was sent into space, beamed at a cluster of stars called M13.
YAWN
But it's so far away we'll have to wait about 50,000 years for a reply.
drum drum
And until we get one...

SPACE STATIONS
In 1971, the USSR launched the first ever space station.
SALYUT 1
In the 1970s and 80s, there was a series of new, improved SALYUTS.
We've been up here for ages.
Longer than the Americans!
Meanwhile, the USA launched its own space station.
SKYLAB (USA)
But...
How are we going to take people there and back?
Err, the SPACE SHUTTLE won't be ready until 1981!
NASA
So Skylab was abandoned in 1974. In 1979 it fell to Earth in Australia ... killing a cow.
URK
The USA decided to build a reusable aircraft instead of more space stations.

The USSR launched a new space station in 1986.
We called it MIR
which means PEACE
We were feeling optimistic.
A Mir cosmonaut holds the world record for the longest period in space.
I'm VALERY POLYAKOV.
I was in orbit for 438 days.
It got a bit dull after the first six months.
But I didn't crack...
Hnnn
Sorry about the nuclear threats and all that.
Let's forgive and forget!
The USSR broke up and everyone was a bit less huffy with one another.
In 1993, Russia joined the USA, CANADA, JAPAN and 11 other countries...
We're all working together...
On the INTERNATIONAL SPACE STATION.
The first bit of the ISS was launched in 1998 and the first crew was sent in 2000.
The crew is changed regularly.
So no one's ever beaten Valery's record.
And we're quite happy about that!

But what if you actually LIVED there?

LIVING IN SPACE

In some ways, living in space can be fun.
Whey-hey
Wheee
In others, it can be really annoying...
SUCK SUCK
Whoops!
My lunch is escaping!
crumbs
Some astronauts suffer from space sickness...
GULP!
But they soon get used to life in space...
Sleeping...
Mm... cosy.
EYE MASK (there's no Earth night and day)
STRAPS (floating about while asleep can cause problems)
Eating...
Mmm... freeze-dried mince again!
LUNCH
DINNE
LUNCH

Exercising...
So we do lots of this to keep fit!
Astronauts on the first space stations came back to Earth very weak because there's no gravity to push against.
Going to the toilet...
Working...
Just off to do a few repairs...
in the terrifying emptiness of space.
Washing...
We try to avoid it as much as possible actually.
NASTY NIFF
And passing the time...
Floating tiddlywinks, anyone?
Not again!
Bet I can stay upside down the longest!

So, what's next?

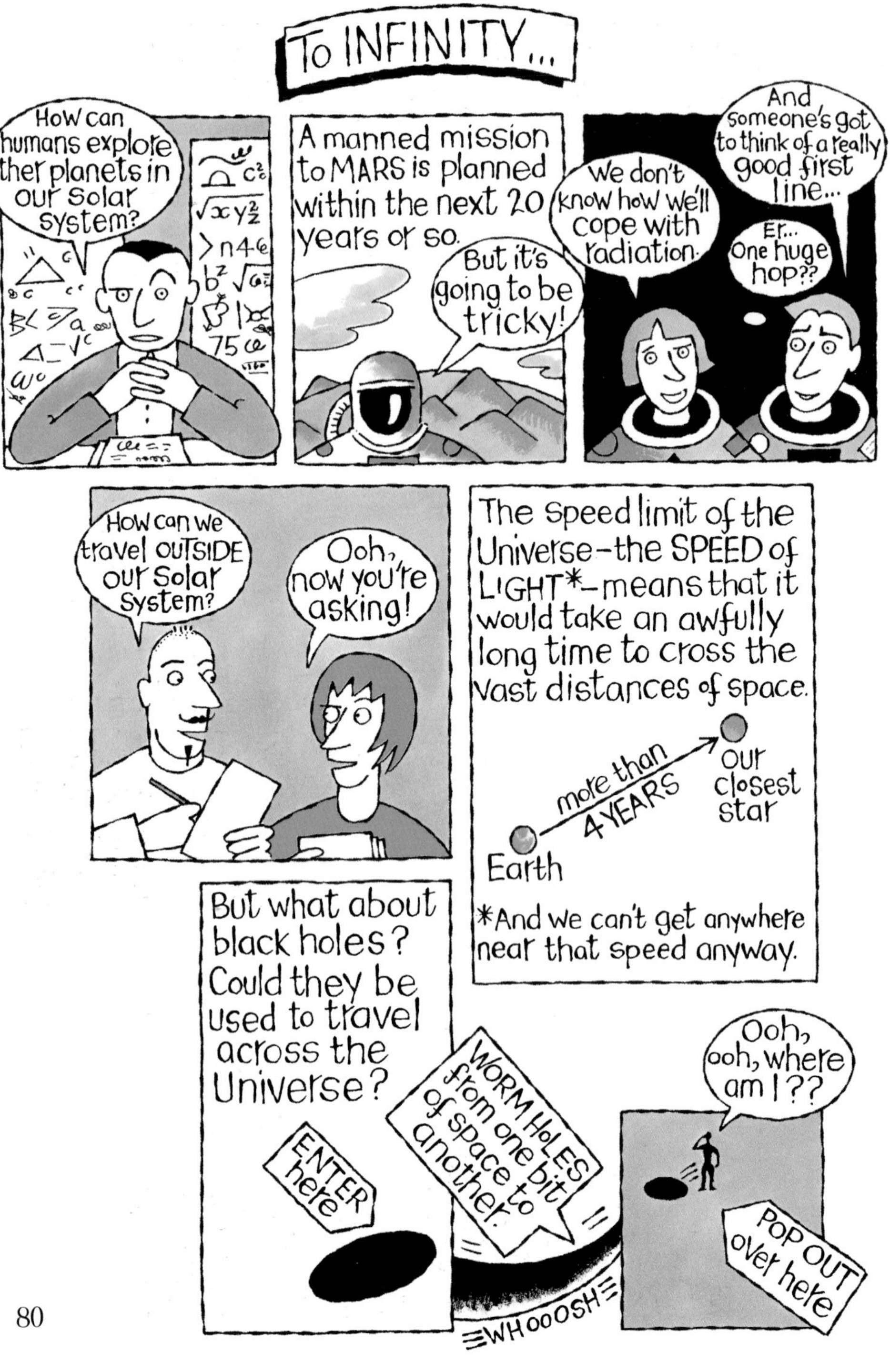
To INFINITY...
How can humans explore other planets in our Solar system?
A manned mission to MARS is planned within the next 20 years or so.
But it's going to be tricky!
We don't know how we'll cope with radiation.
And someone's got to think of a really good first line...
Er... One huge hop??
How can we travel OUTSIDE our Solar System?
Ooh, now you're asking!
The speed limit of the Universe – the SPEED of LIGHT* – means that it would take an awfully long time to cross the vast distances of space.
Earth
more than 4 YEARS
our closest star
*And we can't get anywhere near that speed anyway.
But what about black holes? Could they be used to travel across the Universe?
ENTER here
WORM HOLES from one bit of space to another.
WHOOOSH
Ooh, ooh, where am I??
POP OUT over here

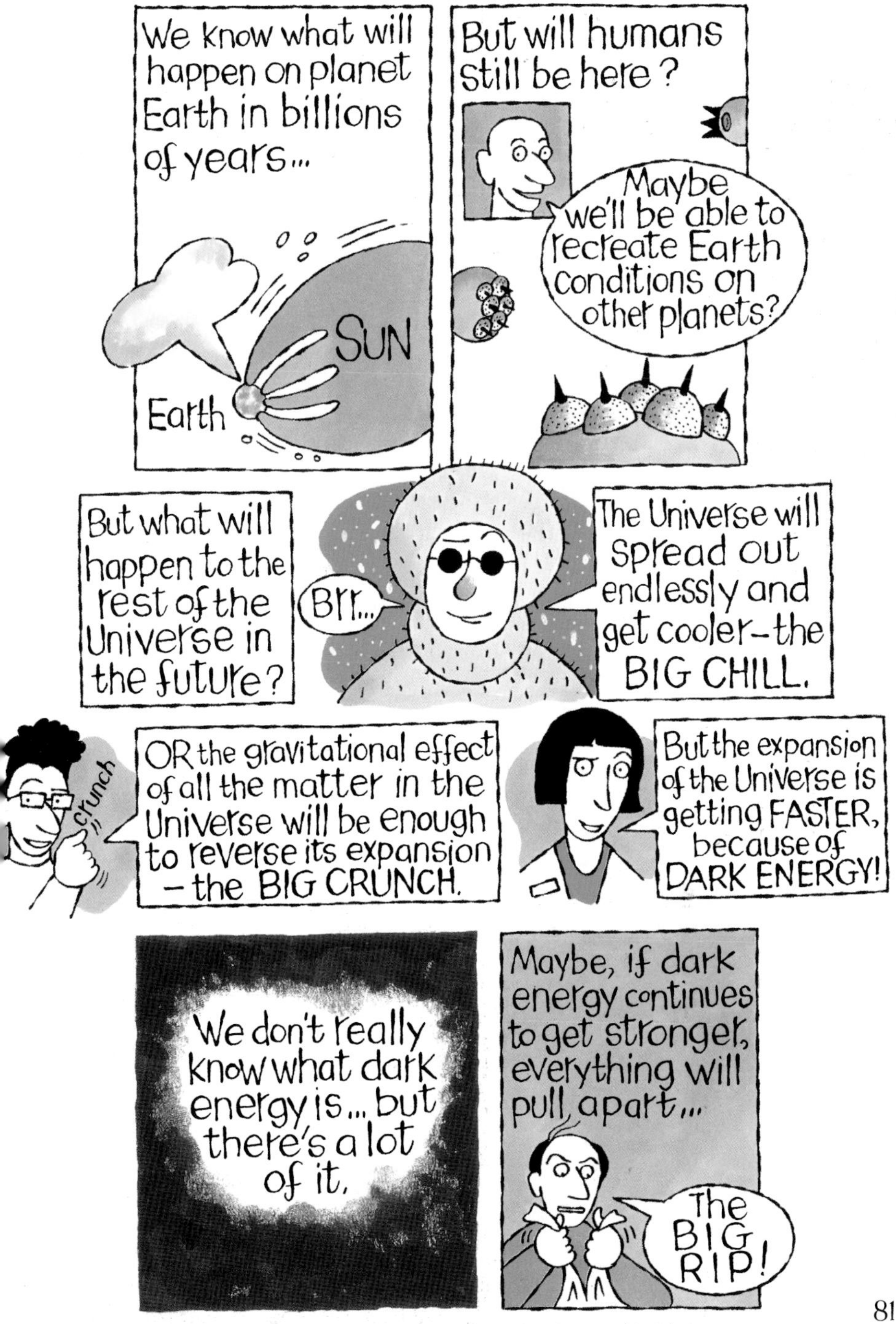
We know what will happen on planet Earth in billions of years...
SUN
Earth
But will humans still be here?
Maybe we'll be able to recreate Earth conditions on other planets?
But what will happen to the rest of the Universe in the future?
Brr...
The Universe will spread out endlessly and get cooler – the BIG CHILL.
crunch
OR the gravitational effect of all the matter in the Universe will be enough to reverse its expansion – the BIG CRUNCH.
But the expansion of the Universe is getting FASTER, because of DARK ENERGY!
We don't really know what dark energy is... but there's a lot of it.
Maybe, if dark energy continues to get stronger, everything will pull apart...
The BIG RIP!

and BEYOND...

Will we ever make contact with intelligent life on other planets?
All over the world, people are listening...
to the furthest reaches of space...
beepa beepa
bleep bleep
tweeta tweet
cheep cheep
blip blop
beep
We're the SETI organisation...
the SEARCH for EXTRATERRESTRIAL INTELLIGENCE.
Yes!
We're listening for radio signals transmitted by ALIEN technology.
Perhaps one day we'll meet some...
or perhaps, given the vastness of space and time, we never shall.

Maybe intelligent alien life has its own SETI and is making sense of our own most common radio transmissions.
And now it's time for TOP GEAR!
!!!!
Oh no, not again!
What's this? Images of... UGGH! A race of horribly ugly, stupid, backward ALIENS!
Gross!
Blah blah
And they always seem to be at WAR...
So last billennium!
Ng!
BAM
BIFF
And have terrible trouble with constipation.
!!!!
LAXI-LOT unblocks your bot
Let's ignore them!
Nng!
Blah blah

and now for **part three . . .**

(featuring minotaurs,
some gods, and a bit of
eye-gouging . . .)

the COMIC STRIP

Greatest Greek Myths

Contents

Murder, Revenge, Monsters, Shipwrecks, Large Wooden Horses, etc. 1
Mythical Monsters: A Who's Who 2
Gods, etc.: A Who's Who 4
In the Beginning 8
Persephone, Queen of the Underworld 10
Prometheus and the Theft of Fire. . . . 12
Pandora's Box 14
The Twelve Labours of Heracles 16
King Midas and the Golden Touch. . . . 22
King Midas and the Ass's Ear 24
Jason and the Argonauts. 26
Sisyphus Cheats Death 32
Atalanta and the Golden Apples 34
The Labours of Theseus. 36
The Flight of Icarus. 44
Narcissus and Echo 46
Perseus and Medusa. 48
Bellerophon and the Flying Horse 54
Orpheus in the Underworld 56
King Tantalus's Punishment. 58

King Oedipus 60
Helen of Troy 62
The Trojan War Begins 64
Achilles' Heel 66
The Wooden Horse of Troy 68
The Murder of Agamemnon 70
The Voyages of Odysseus 72
The Greeks and Romans (and everyone else) 78

MURDER, REVENGE, MONSTERS, SHIPWRECKS, LARGE WOODEN HORSES ETC...

People have always told stories. Some explain the natural world . . .
Persephone's come up from the Underworld, I see.
Others explain the way people behave.

The Ancient Greeks told some of the best stories ever, full of . . .

Eye-gouging!
Baby-eating!
Hic!
Slurp!
hissss!
Stump-scorching!
Liver-pecking!
Oh!
My turn!
Tooth-sharing!
Ow!
Three-headed dogs!
Don't forget the heroic deeds!
Our myths have been told for nearly 3,000 years . . .
And STILL no one's come up with anything more heroic . . .
Or alarming!
Or gruesome!
Let's introduce ourselves . . .

MYTHICAL MONSTERS:

We're fun-loving friends of the wine god, Dionysus.

SATYR

We're more friends of Dionysus.
We can be violent.
Hnn.

CENTAUR

Mama!
Keep still, Hydra!
I'm the monstrous mother of Cerberus, the Hydra, the Chimera, the Sphinx and the Nemean Lion . . . phew!

THE ECHIDNA

I'm Stheno.
I'm Euryale.
I'm Medusa.
Anyone who looks at us is turned to stone!

THE GORGONS

Coo-ee, sailor!
Tra-la-la
Heh heh!

SIRENS

A WHO'S WHO

I'm off to terrorise the people of Lycia.

THE CHIMERA

We're three ancient sisters. We share one eye and one tooth!

THE GRAEAE

You'd better get the right answer to my riddle . . . or else!
Grrr.

THE SPHINX

Woof!
Grr!
Snarl!

CERBERUS

We carry victims off to the Underworld.
No, no!
Cackle cackle
We steal food too.

THE HARPIES

Hnnn

CYCLOPS

GODS ETC.
A WHO'S WHO
I'm the top god, and these are my brothers and sisters.
We're called the Olympian gods, because we live on Mount Olympus.
ZEUS
Ouch!
I'm god of the sea.
POSEIDON
I'm the harvest goddess.
DEMETER
I'm the hunter goddess.
ARTEMIS
I'm god of wine.
Hic!
S'cuse me.
DIONYSUS
I'm god of the sun, archery and music.
Tum ti tum
APOLLO
I'm the warrior goddess of wisdom.
ATHENE

I'm Zeus's wife and queen of the gods.
HERA
I'm goddess of love and beauty.
APHRODITE
I'm Demeter's daughter and queen of the Underworld.
PERSEPHONE
I'm the blacksmith god of fire and volcanoes.
HEPHAESTOS
I'm the messenger god.
Must fly (ahem).
HERMES
I'm god of war.
Grr, gnash, etc.
ARES
I'm king of the Underworld. Heh heh!
HADES
I'm goddess of the home.
Cup of tea?
As well as us very important gods, there are minor gods . . .
and even some important human heroes . . .
HESTIA

WHO'S WHO (CONTINUED)
We're beautiful nature spirits.
Some of us are immortal . . .
Urk
NYMPHS
I'm god of goatherds and shepherds.
Toot toot!
PAN
We're goddesses of art, music, poetry and science.
There are nine of us.
THE MUSES
I'm goddess of strife.
Nng!
ERIS
I spin the thread of every human life . . .
I decide how long it is.
And I cut it!
Cackle!
Tee hee
THE FATES

I shoot arrows of love or indifference.
Depends on my mood.
EROS
We relentlessly pursue unpunished criminals.
Revenge!
Hnn!
THE FURIES
We're fierce warrior women.
Grr!
AMAZONS
I'm goddess of victory.
NIKE
We're mortal men, usually with a divine parent or two.
Strong!
Brave!
And modest!
HERACLES
THESEUS
ODYSSEUS
ACHILLES
JASON
PERSEUS
BELLEROPHON
THE HEROES
I'm one of the TITANS, an older race of gods, defeated by the Olympians . . .

IN THE BEGINNING...

CHAOS
Then there was . . .
the Earth.
the Underworld
And a race of gods.
We're the Titans.
Some of us have baby Titans.
Wah! wah!
Not me, though.
Hnn
I'm Kronos.
clench clench
I EAT my babies in case they try to overthrow me - better safe than sorry!
Wah, wah!
Munch!
I'm Rhea, Kronos's wife.
I'm getting a bit fed up with this. I'm going to trick Kronos.

stone
He'll never notice the difference.
Here you are.
Yum!
Hic!
That one was a bit crunchy.
I'll call him Zeus.
Gurgle.
Years later . . . Kronos had been right to be careful . . .
I'm Zeus.
Ha! You ate my brothers and sisters.
Nng!
Squeeze squeeze
Aarggh! I knew you didn't taste right!
I defeated the Titans, made Kronos regurgitate my brothers and sisters, moved to Mount Olympus and became ruler of everything!
Hnn
It's about time for a different myth – and this one's all about me . . .

PERSEPHONE QUEEN OF THE UNDERWORLD

I'm Demeter, and this is my lovely daughter Persephone.
Aww, MUM!
One day . . .
Tra la la...
Ho!
Aargh! It's Hades, god of the Underworld!
You brute! Help!
You're coming with me!
Will you marry me, the way?
Demeter searched for Persephone everywhere.
Persephone! Where are you?
Demeter was too busy searching to make the seasons happen.
Urk

We can't have this. Demeter, stop moping and change the season.
Sigh!
Right-o, Zeus.
Hnnn
No one who has eaten food here can ever leave the Underworld.
Hermes, go and get Persephone from the Underworld.
Here, have something to eat!
Heh heh heh!
Persephone ate some pomegranate seeds in the Underworld.
Ha! That means you can't return to the world of the living!
Tee hee
Aargh!
STAGGER STAGGER
Does that mean I've had a wasted journey?
As a compromise, from then on, Persephone spent nine months with her mother . . .
. . . And three months with Hades.
And while she's down there, it's winter up here.

PROMETHEUS AND THE THEFT OF FIRE

The Titans who had fought against Zeus were banished to the Underworld.
What a drag.
Yawn yawn.
I'm SO bored.
The others were allowed to stay.
Like me, Prometheus.
I'm still a bit miffed with Zeus, though, so I'm going to help out the weedy mortals for a bit.
Men! I demand a sacrifice.
An ox would be nice.
We'd better be nice to powerful Zeus!
Thanks. We gods will have all the lovely meaty bits . . .
and you lot can have the bones and yucky innards.
Eh?
Let's trick the old meanie!
gruesome bits
Yeah!
Eugh!
Prometheus and those puny men have tricked me! How can I get my revenge?
Oooh, I know!

Brrr.
It's so cold and dark.
Zeus has taken fire away from us.
Don't worry, men! I've stolen some fire from the god Hephaestos.
Here you are!
Right, that does it! Now I'm really cross.
As a punishment, Zeus had Prometheus chained to a rock. Every day an eagle came and pecked out his liver . . .
Oh dear!
. . . which would then grow back in time for the eagle's lunch the next day.
Yum!
TUG TUG
squelch
Ouch
Not again!
Don't worry – one day I'm saved by Heracles.
Now, how am I going to get my revenge on the men? Oooh, I know . . .

PANDORA'S BOX

Hephaestos, create a woman for me, would you?
A WHAT?
A woman. Like a man, but cleverer and more beautiful.
Hmm . . . This isn't going to be easy . . .
Ooh
Off you go, Pandora! To inflict my terrible revenge on mankind.
Heh heh
Hello! Are you Epimetheus, Prometheus's brother?
I'm a gift from Zeus.
Gosh. How nice.
I know Prometheus warned me not to accept gifts from the gods . . .
But what harm can it do?
I always cry at weddings!
I say!
What a stunner!

I can't resist . . .
. . . I'm only human.
To P and E
Congratulations! Love, ZEUS XXX
DO NOT OPEN!

DISEASE
POVERTY
EVIL
OTHER NASTY STUFF
HOPE
DO NOT OPEN!

THE TWELVE LABOURS OF HERACLES

Heracles was a Greek hero.
Hnnn!
But Hera, queen of the gods, didn't like Heracles and made him go mad.
Nng.
In my madness, I killed my family.
As a punishment, he was sent to serve Eurystheus, King of Tiryns.
I'm going to give you a task every year for 12 years.
Oh?
Right-o.
Here's the first one: Kill the Nemean Lion.
Labour 1: Kill the Nemean Lion.
Grr . . .
Urk!
Grr . . .
THROTTLE
THROTTLE
Lion's hide impervious to weapons
That wasn't so bad.
Smart!
And the skin will make a great weapon-proof cloak!

Labour 2: Kill the Lernaean Hydra.
Gaaa! Every time I chop off a head, two new ones grow back!
Aha! Burning the stumps stops them growing back!
Hisss
Phew! This one's immortal, so I have to bury it.
Labour 3: Capture the Ceryneian Hind.
Labour 4: Capture the Erymanthian Boar.

Labour 5:
Clean the Augean Stables.
Problem: lots of poo.
Solution: 2 rivers cunningly diverted
WHOOSH
Labour 6:
Drive away the Stymphalian Birds.
CLACK
CLACK
Bronze castanets to scare birds from trees (a gift from Athene).
bronze wings
bronze beaks and claws
Urk
Urk

Labour 7: Capture the Cretan Bull.
Urk
Ha!
Labour 8: Steal the Mares of King Diomedes.
Killing the guards is the easy part . . .
Urk
Whinny
Gnash Gnash
Hmm, dinner!
It's the man-eating horses you have to watch out for . . .
Snort
Nnnn
I find they're much calmer after a good meal.
Muzzles to stop horses eating anyone on the way home.
Gee up!
Spoilsport!

Labour 9: Fetch the Girdle of the Queen of the Amazons.
Come on, Hippolyte, hand it over.
Get lost!
girdle
I tried asking nicely.
Heh heh
Urk
Labour 10: Capture the Cattle of Geryon.
Gah!
Hnnn.
Slaver
Moo
Snarl
That's Geryon. But I managed to kill him and his dog and nick his cattle!

Labour 11: Fetch the Apples of the Hesperides.
Hmm . . .
Zzz . . .
Atlas, if I kill the dragon, would you get the apples?
I'll hold up the heavens while you're gone.
All right, then.
I could do with a break and the Hesperides are my daughters.
Got them!
Labour 12: Bring Cerberus from the Underworld.
Fetching Hell's hound wasn't easy, I can tell you!
That's the last task – now I'm off to have a bath.
Yelp
Whimper
Growl

KING MIDAS AND THE GOLDEN TOUCH

Three million, one thousand and thirty-five . . .
Your Most Royal Wonderfulness, sir . . .
gold tooth
What? Oh blast! I've lost count. I'll have to start again . . . one, two . . .
But your Most Fabulous Highness, sir . . .
Five . . . Oh, yes. What is it?
Come into the rose garden, Your Royal Marvellousness. There seems to be a satyr in it.
Hic! Hnnn
Oh, that's Silenus. He's a big pal of the wine god Dionysus. We'd better be nice to him.
Do tell me another of your stories, Silenus.
Clink
More wine?
Don't mind if I do!
This IS fun!
Midas, I thank you for looking after my friend.
In return, I grant you one wish. What do you fancy?
Hmmm . . .
Ooh, I know! I wish that everything I touch would turn to gold!

How lovely!
gleam
gleam
Bother! I'll have to smell my roses without touching them.
Ping!
gleam
I feel a bit peckish. Oh no!
Hello, lovely daughter. Oh no!
Ping!
gleam
Dionysus! Please get me out of this mess!
Oh, all right, then. Go and bathe in the river Pactolus.
splish splash
I hope this works!
From now on I'm not going to be so greedy. I might even share things a bit more!
Hooray!
Hooray!
Hooray!

KING MIDAS AND THE ASS'S EARS

I'm the best musician in the world, ever.
"toot toot"
Oi! I heard that, Marsyas, you cheeky satyr!
No one is a better musician than me, the god Apollo!
Right! Let's have a competition and find out, shall we?
Pah! You think you can play better than a god, do you? The nerve!
Tum ti tum!
I'm SO glad that everything I touch doesn't turn into gold any more. I like music better than money these days. I hear there's a contest between some satyr and the god Apollo - must go along . . .
tootle toot
strum strum
Apollo is the winner!
Yay!
Hurrah!
Well done, Your Godliness!
I thought the satyr was better, actually.

What did you say, King Midas?
Gulp!
Oh, nothing, really. Just . . . you know . . .
There must be something wrong with your ears!
Oh no! I'll have to wear this cap to hide them!
Listen, barber, don't breathe a word of this - on pain of death!
I can't stand it any longer . . .
King Midas has ass's ears!
Later, reeds grew where the barber had dug the hole.
King Midas has ass's ears!
rustle rustle
King Midas has ass's ears!
Did you hear that? Quick! Let's spread the gossip!
I guess the secret's out. Now, where's that barber?
Chortle
Har har
Tee hee
Tee hee
Ho ho

JASON AND THE ARGONAUTS

My uncle, King Pelias, has promised me his kingdom of Iolcus if I can fetch the Golden Fleece from Colchis.
We're the Argonauts, here to help our pal, Jason.
Including me, the hero Heracles.
Then the Argonauts had to fight off the horrible food-stealing Harpies.
The Argo only just managed to get through these deadly crashing rocks.
whump
Iolcus
AEGEAN SEA

And me, Orpheus, the famous lyre player.
And me, Atalanta, the only woman on board.
I've been made with magic speaking timber!
BLACK SEA
Colchis
Target: the Golden Fleece
Heracles cleared the land of giants at Cyzicus
Urk

When the Argonauts arrived at Colchis, the King of Colchis set Jason a task.
I'll give you the Golden Fleece if you plough and sow a field for me . . .
I bet there's a catch.
Of course, you'll have to use my bronze-footed, fire-breathing bulls, sow the field with dragon's teeth, and kill the warriors that sprout from them.
Gulp
I'm Medea, the king's daughter, and I can help . . .
Whisper whisper
I say!
Medea gave me a magic potion to protect me from the bulls' fiery breath!
Hnnn
Snort
Snort
Then she told me to throw a rock at the warriors to make them fight and kill each other . . .
. . . and it worked!
CLANG
Nnk!
Nnk!

The Golden Fleece was guarded by a fierce dragon. Medea gave the dragon a magic potion to make it sleep.
ZZZ
Let's scarper! I can claim the throne of Iolcus now.
And I'm coming with you, handsome.

But the Argo's journey back to Iolcus wasn't easy . . .
We were shipwrecked!
So we had to carry the Argo overland for a bit.
Phew!
Yoo hoo!
Then we had to get away from the Sirens' song.
Otherwise they'd have eaten us!
Luckily, my playing was better than their singing and we escaped.
twang twang
Nng
This is so typical!
Medea gave the giant a magic potion.
Zzz
Urk
And I worked out that taking out this nail will kill him!

When Jason arrived in Iolcus . . .
Evil King Pelias killed my parents while I was gone!
What a rotter! Don't worry, Jason, I'll sort him out.
You're King Pelias's daughters, aren't you?
Would you like to help your father live for ever?
Oh yes, lovely!
If you chop up an old ram and put it in here . . .
Look! The ram is restored to a lamb!
Meh
They tried the same magic on Pelias . . .
Oh dear!
I wonder why?
Heh heh
It doesn't seem to have worked!
But there was no happy ending for Jason and Medea:
The trouble I went to, and this is the thanks I get!
Pah!
I abandoned her in the end.

Sisyphus Cheats Death

Bother! I've annoyed Zeus and now the god of the Underworld has come for me.
Come on, Sisyphus, your time's up. Down to the Underworld for your everlasting punishment.
Whoooosh
Pssht
Er . . .
Are those handcuffs, Hades?
Yes, and I'll use them if I have to.
How do they work, then?
A short time later . . .
Then they lock like this, you see . . . oh. You've tricked me, you annoying little man!
CLICK!
No one could die while Hades was imprisoned. Eventually, Ares came to his rescue.
Honestly, that was a bit silly of you.
Nng
Nnk
Right, now you're jolly well coming to the Underworld. And no tricks!

SIGH
That's my husband dead, then. But something tells me he'll be back. He told me not to bury his body . . .
. . . so I'll just have to go back up there and make her bury me!
Hmm.
Yes, I suppose there's nothing else for it.
Hello, Merope!
I knew you'd be back!
Sisyphus lived happily to a ripe old age.
But now I'm ill and actually ready to die.
Bad luck. This time you're really for it. See that rock?
Sisyphus was condemned to roll a great rock to the top of a hill, only for it to roll back down again, for all eternity.
Urgh! This is SO boring!

ATALANTA AND THE GOLDEN APPLES

Atalanta was left to die on a hillside . . .
Wah, wah . . .
. . . but was found by an unusual rescuer . . .
Hnn
Goo goo
After a start like that, it's no surprise that I've grown up as hard as nails!
And one thing's for sure: I'm not marrying some wimp!
Go on, I'm really nice!
Please, Atalanta!
No, me!
All right. I'll marry anyone who can beat me in a race . . .
Sounds fun.
What a stunner!
. . . and anyone who loses has to die!
Eek
Yikes

FINISH
Oh dear. Another one bites the dust.
Gasp, gasp
I feel like meddling in the world of mortals.
Oi, Hippomenes!
Good grief! It's the goddess of love, Aphrodite!
Take these golden apples to distract her, then you'll win the race.
Gosh!
Oooh, what's that?
You won, so let's get married – actually, I quite fancy you.
But Atalanta and Hippomenes didn't live happily ever after . . .
We offended Zeus.
Grr
So he turned us into lions.

THE LABOURS OF THESEUS

It's about time I told you, Theseus. You're really the son of Aegeus, King of Athens!
Mother! You mean . . . I'm a prince? I always knew it!
Your father said to lift this rock, take what's underneath it and go to Athens.
rock
Uhh
Theseus set off for Athens in a heroic mood . . .
Hng
Oi, Periphetes! You can't go around killing travellers . . .
clunk
That'll teach him.
Har har
Oi, Sinis! What do you think you're doing?
PING!

PING!
Serves you right, Sinis!
Hurrah for Theseus!
And now I'm just going to get rid of this monstrous sow -it's been terrorising the neighbourhood for years.
What a rotter!
Hnn
Nng
Hnn
Nng
I offer travellers either this short bed for the night or this long one. I just cut them or stretch them to fit!
Har har!
Not another evil-doer!
Gosh, I'm so heroic. Next stop, Athens!
Urk

Athens at last! Now all I have to do is find my father . . .
King Aegeus's wife was Medea the sorceress.
Hnn
I'm going to stop Theseus from telling his father who he is and ruining my own son's chances!
Husband! A deadly assassin has arrived to kill you!
Gosh!
Let's poison him!
You know best, dear.
We'll invite him to a feast . . .
Heh heh
THESEUS
Cheers.
STOP! Those sandals and that sword it's my son!

Awww . . .
Dad!
And as for you, Medea, you evil, scheming witch, consider yourself banished!
Bother.
Snort
Bellow
Oh, that's the monstrous bull that keeps killing people.
What's that?
Right!
Urgh!
He won't be bothering the people of Athens any more!
That reminds me, Theseus. Every nine years the people of Athens are forced to send seven boys and seven girls to King Minos of Crete, who feeds them to a bull-headed monster that lives in a maze.
Gulp!
Sort it out for us, would you?

Erm . . . this way?
Yikes
Argh! What was that?

I want my mum!
MINOTAUR
Snort
BELLOW!
Anyone there?
THESEUS

Theseus was helped in his quest to kill the Minotaur by Ariadne, King Minos's daughter.
I'm in love!
Daedalus, you made the labyrinth, so you've got to help!
I'm sure Theseus can kill the Minotaur, but how will he get out of the labyrinth?
I'd love to help. I can't stand King Minos. He won't get out without this.
Take this special ball of wool – leave a trail and you'll find a way out.
Gosh, thanks.
You lot stay here. I'm off to kill the Minotaur. Back in a tick.

AARGH
AARGH
Ouch!
Urk
Thanks to Ariadne's ball of wool, we found our way out.
Hooray!
Come on, everyone! To the ships!
Bye!!
King Minos, Your Most Wonderful Highness, sire . . . I'm afraid the Minotaur is dead, and Theseus has got away and taken Ariadne with him!
Curses!

THE FLIGHT OF ICARUS
King Minos imprisoned Daedalus and his son, Icarus, for helping Theseus escape the Labyrinth.
Come on, Dad. Think of something!
King Minos has guards everywhere . . . on land . . .
Grr
Hnn
. . . and at sea . . .
Nng
Grr
So that just leaves . . . Got it!
Remember, Icarus, when you put these on, just follow me and DON'T FLY TOO CLOSE TO THE SUN! Or the wax will melt and the wings will fall apart.
Gosh!

But Icarus DID fly too close to the sun. He crashed into the sea and drowned.

NARCISSUS AND ECHO

Echo the nymph had upset the goddess Hera.
You naughty nymph! You're so fond of chatting . . .
But from now on you'll only be able to repeat someone else's words.
You great big meanie!
One day, Echo noticed a beautiful young man.
Oooh, there goes Narcissus. What a dreamboat.
I'm in love!
Is anybody here?
Here!
Snap! rustle rustle
Where are you?
Where are you?
Come here!
Come here!
Aargh! Get off! I'm not interested, love.

Poor Echo pined away, until only her voice remained.
Coo-ee!
Coo-ee!
Look, I know I'm gorgeous, but will you please just GO AWAY!
Gods! It's time that arrogant Narcissus was punished.
All right. I'll make him fall in love with someone he can't have.
Help me, Artemis, hunter goddess!
I say, who's that?
Narcissus had fallen in love with his own reflection.
Eventually he pined away, until only a beautiful flower remained in his place.

PERSEUS AND MEDUSA

The King of Seriphos invited the island's noblemen to a feast.
All of you have to give me a horse.
Of course, Your Royalness!
Only one?
A pleasure, sire!
Straight away, Your Greatness.
Sorry, King. I can't afford a horse – you might as well ask me for a Gorgon's head!
All right, then, Perseus.
Bring me the head of the Gorgon Medusa – the hideous monster that turns people to stone with one glance.
I've never liked him anyway.
Bother. I've landed myself in it now.
Cheer up! Here's a shield. Look at Medusa's reflection in it when you cut off her head.
And here's a special head-chopping sword.
Thanks, Athene and Hermes!
No one knows where they live – except their sisters, the Graeae.
But you need to find the Stygian nymphs – they have other things you need.
This is complicated!

We're the Graeae.
We only have one eye between us!
And one tooth!
Cackle cackle
Hello, Graeae. I'm looking for your sisters.
We're not telling YOU where to find them!
No way!
Never!
OK, no more Mr Nice Guy.
Straight up the road!
First left!
Nng!
Then right at the oak tree . . .

Hello.
Are you the Stygian nymphs?
At your service. You'll need this Cap of Invisibility.
That should come in handy.
And these Winged Sandals.
flip flap
I've always wanted a pair of those!
And this leather bag. It's to put Medusa's head in once you've chopped it off.
Thanks, nymphs!
flip flap
Wheee!

Ssss
Ssss
Ssss
Nnng

That wasn't so difficult after all. Mind you, I did have a bit of help.

Whinny!
I'm Pegasus and I sprang from Medusa's blood.
Snort

Meanwhile, after killing Medusa, Perseus was still feeling heroic . . .
What's that?
Help!

Andromeda was being sacrificed because her mother had boasted that they were fairer than the sea nymphs.
Fear not, beautiful woman!
Argh
Quick, get away while you still can! A sea monster's coming to eat me!

Take that!
Nng!
Just a couple of things before we can live happily ever after, Andromeda.
Urk
Crack!
Here's your Gorgon's head, you mean old king!
Crack!
Aaar-
Thanks, Athene. Would you like the head?
Cheers, Perseus. I'll use it to turn my enemies to stone.

BELLEROPHON AND THE FLYING HORSE

Bellerophon was given a task by the King of Lycia . . .

Would you mind destroying the Chimera? It's being an awful nuisance
What's the Chimera?
Hnn!
Urk
HOWL
Oh, just a sort of . . . lion-goat-y, dragon-snake-y sort of thing.
This is going to be tricky. I'll consult a fortune teller.
Nng!
Bellerophon! Here's a tip for you: tame the winged horse, Pegasus – he'll help you!
Pegasus lived with the Muses of Mount Helicon.
That was easy!
Whinny!

Bellerophon and Pegasus defeated the Chimera together . . .
Urk
Then Bellerophon got a bit cocky.
Come on, Pegasus! We'll fly to Mount Olympus!
Oh no you won't!
Aaarrggh!
Zeus made Pegasus into a constellation.
And sometimes I help Zeus with his thunderbolts.

ORPHEUS IN THE UNDERWORLD
I'm Orpheus, the most famous poet and musician ever.
Even I, the great god Apollo, recognise your talent.
Wow! Thanks, Apollo.
Gosh!
I'm Eurydice.
We're so in love!
Soon afterwards . . .
Ow!
Urk
Oh no!
Right, I'm just going to have to get her back from the Underworld.

This must e the River Styx. he dead have to ross it to get to the Underworld.
Sorry, you're not dead.
Will you take me across, ferryman?
Oh, all right then.
Your music has put me, Hades, ferocious god of the Underworld, in a good mood.
What can I do for you?
drool
yip
whimper
Hades, please let me take Eurydice back up to the land of the living.
Go on, then. But you mustn't look back till Eurydice is in the sunlight again, or she'll be lost for ever.
I might just have a peek.
You complete twit, Orpheus! Goodbye for ever!

KING TANTALUS'S PUNISHMENT

King Tantalus was the only human allowed to dine with the gods.
Pass the nectar, would you, Tantalus?
Top up?
Cheersh!
Have some of this! It's ambrosia and nectar, the food and drink of the gods!
Ooooh, yummy!
Bye, then, gods and goddesses. See you next week!
And have you heard the latest about Zeus and Hera?
WHISPER WHISPER
Tantalus, we know you nicked some of our grub. AND we know you've been gossiping!
Don't punish me! Come to a special feast at my place!

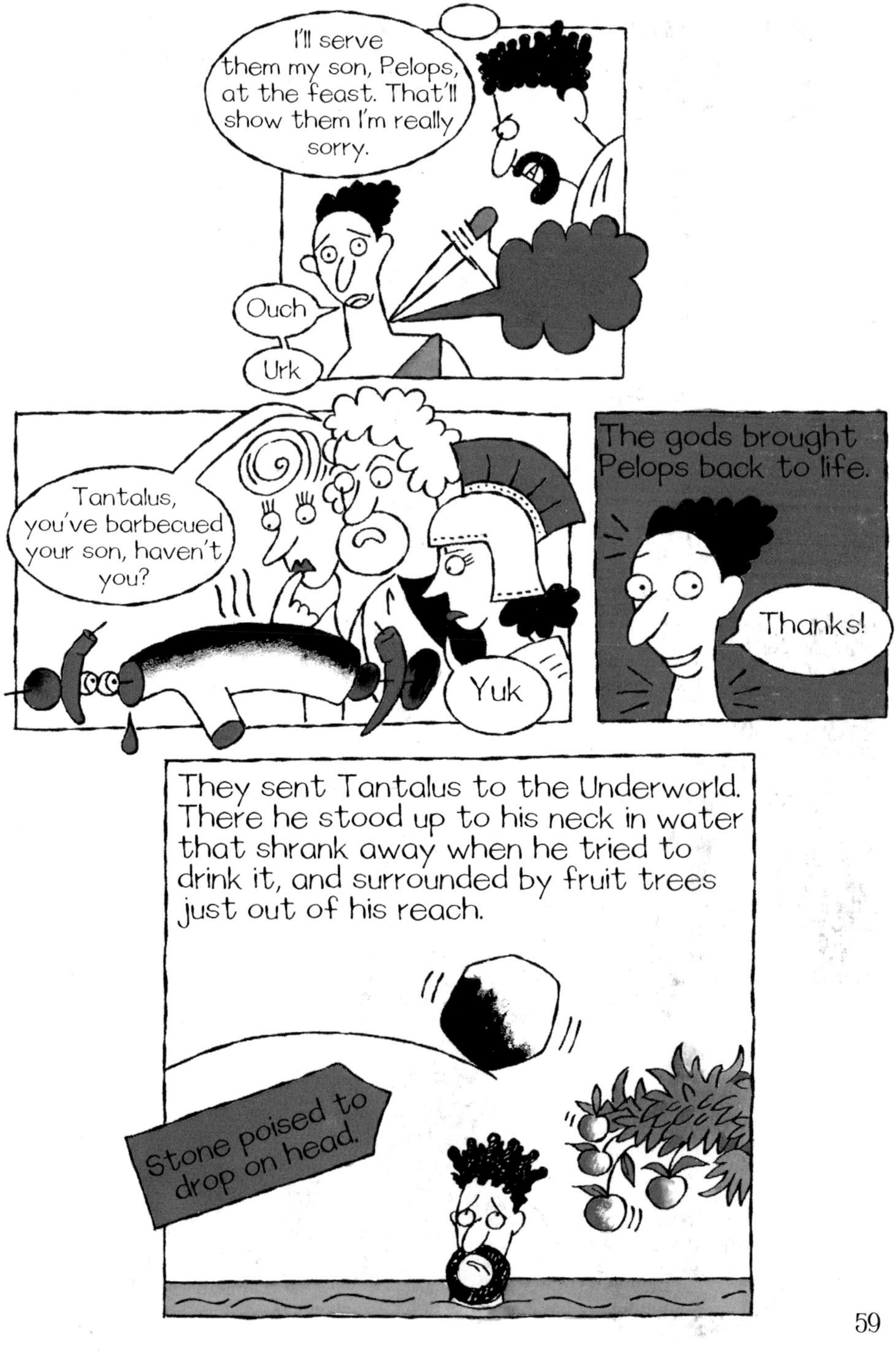
I'll serve them my son, Pelops, at the feast. That'll show them I'm really sorry.
Ouch
Urk
Tantalus, you've barbecued your son, haven't you?
Yuk
The gods brought Pelops back to life.
Thanks!
They sent Tantalus to the Underworld. There he stood up to his neck in water that shrank away when he tried to drink it, and surrounded by fruit trees just out of his reach.
Stone poised to drop on head.

KING OEDIPUS

King Laius of Thebes left his son to die because of a prophecy that the child would grow up and kill him.
Wah, wah
You poor thing! I'll take you with me to Corinth. I'll call you Oedipus.
Goo goo!
Years later, Oedipus was walking to Thebes, when . . .
Out of my way, peasant!
Oi!
Take that!
Urk!
Then his day got even worse . . .
I am the Sphinx and I've a riddle for you. If you don't get it right, I'll throttle you!
What has four feet in the morning, two legs at midday and three legs in the evening?
That's easy! A man! He crawls as a baby, then walks on two legs, and leans on a staff in old age.
Curses!
Urk

As his prize for getting rid of the Sphinx, Oedipus was made king of Thebes.
I'm Queen Jocasta.
My husband died recently. I'll marry you instead!
All was well until one day a prophet arrived at the palace.
Oedipus! You have killed your father and married your mother!
Nonsense! My father's a shepherd, I haven't seen my mother in ages, and I haven't killed anyone!
Oh, apart from that traveller on the way to Thebes!
The shepherd isn't your father. He found you on a hillside.
Oh no! The traveller you killed was my husband. And YOU are the baby we abandoned!
!!!!!
I'm off to wander the world as a lonely, blind beggar.
We're the Furies, fearsome goddesses who avenge unpunished crimes.
And we're going to follow you!

HELEN OF TROY

I'm Eris, goddess of strife.
GNASH
And if there's one thing I can't stand, it's not being invited to big, posh weddings!
Love the hat!
Oh, dahling, thank you.
So Eris sent a golden apple to the wedding feast.
For the Fairest
It's mine!
A mortal man shall judge whether Hera, Athene or Aphrodite is the most beautiful . . .
I appoint you, Paris, Prince of Troy!
Thanks a lot, Zeus.

Pick me, Hera, queen of the gods, and I'll make you a powerful king!
Choose me, Athene, warrior goddess, and I promise you'll win any battle you fight!
Choose me, Aphrodite, goddess of love, and I'll give you the most beautiful woman in the world!
It's a difficult decision, but . . . Aphrodite, you're the fairest!
simper simper
Aphrodite had forgotten to mention that the world's most beautiful woman, Helen, was already married to someone else.
Yes! To me, King Menelaus of Sparta. After he'd chosen Aphrodite, Paris came and stole Helen from me.
Grrr
And I'm really cross about it!
I'm Helen of Troy now. But Menelaus is very cross indeed . . .

THE TROJAN WAR BEGINS

Agamemnon, the Trojans have taken my wife! This is an insult to all Greeks!
No one steals my brother's wife! We must be avenged!
Nng
TROY
GREECE
SPARTA
This means WAR!
Let's round up a Greek fleet and set sail for Troy!
TROY
The goddess Artemis is on the Trojans' side. She's making the winds blow the wrong way.
So I'm sacrificing my daughter, Iphigenia, to make the gods change the wind.
This is SO unfair.

TROY
It worked!
Grrr
Nng!
Haarrgghh!
Watch out, Trojans!
BIFF
WHACK
BASH
URK

The Greeks besieged the city of Troy for ten years.

Achilles' Heel

Achilles was the son of Thetis the sea-nymph.
Mama!
If only I could make you immortal like me. Hang on, I've got an idea!
Thetis dipped Achilles in the River Styx in the Underworld.
No harm can come to you where the Styx water has touched you.
Unfortunately, I have to hang on to you, so the water hasn't touched your heel. Oh, never mind – I'm sure it won't matter!
Wah!
We are the Fates, Achilles, goddesses of destiny!
You have grown into a fine young man.
Gosh.
Now we offer you a choice . . .
A short and glorious life . . .
Or a long and uneventful one?
A short and glorious one, of course!

Achilles became the best Greek warrior fighting in the Trojan War.
Haarrgghh! Take that, Trojans!
Urk
Great god Apollo, you're on the Trojans' side. Can't you help?
I'm fed up with that Achilles. He's killing all the Trojan soldiers and he never seems to get hurt.
Yes, he's getting on my nerves too. Fire an arrow at him and I'll help you.
Heh heh!
Urk
Oh no! What are we going to do without mighty Achilles?
Hmmm . . . I'm Odysseus and I've got an idea . . .

THE WOODEN HORSE OF TROY

The Greek warrior Odysseus had a cunning plan . . .
DING!
Everyone likes a nice present.
Ha!
HUGE HORSE MADE of WOOD
Where are all the Greeks?
Hurray! The war's over!
An offering to Athene from the Greeks
They must have all gone home!
Because the Trojans think the horse is a gift for Athene, they bring it inside the city.

Good grief!
What a lovely present!
Greek soldiers hidden in here
Move up a bit!
Ow!
That's
y foot!
Shhh!
Odysseus's plan worked: the Greek warriors came out of the horse in the dead of night, sacked the city of Troy and won the war.
BIFF
Nng!
Urk
BASH
Urk
Hooray!
We're the best!

THE MURDER OF AGAMEMNON

After the Trojan War, King Agamemnon and the other Greek warriors sailed back home.
It's been ten years since I was at home in Argos. Can't wait to see my wife, Queen Clytemnestra.
I'm Queen Clytemnestra. Me and my new boyfriend, Aegisthus, rule Argos now.
Heh heh
And we've got a surprise for Agamemnon.
Hello, Agamemnon. Perhaps you'd like a nice bath after your long journey?
Oooh, that'd be great!
That's for sacrificing my daughter, Iphigenia!
Yes! Har har!
What a welcome!
Urk

Orestes was Agamemnon and Clytemnestra's son.
I have to avenge my father's death. I've been away from the family for so long that Aegisthus and my mother won't recognise me . . .
Gah!
Urk
Urk
We're after you, Orestes!
Woo!!!
Boo!!!
You can't get away with killing your own mother!
Nng
Argh
The Furies are driving me mad!
We need to sort this out. Orestes, you'll be put on trial . . .
Of course, great goddess Athene.
What could be worse than being chased by those scary Furies?
And I will be judge. Well, I am goddess of wisdom. Orestes can go free!
Boo!
Curses!
Phew!

THE VOYAGES OF ODYSSEUS

After the Trojan War, the Greek warrior Odysseus set off back home to Ithaca.
On the way . . .
I sent some men off to explore this island ages ago. Honestly! I'll have to go and fetch them.
We're the Lotus Eaters!
We've given your men lotus juice!
And now we just want to lie around drinking it.
SLURP
Come on, you lazy lot!
Come on!
We'll never get home at this rate.
Hnn!
Look! An island with lots of sheep on it!
Let's stop and buy some and have a huge feast!
Hurray!

Baa!
Gaaaa! Sheep-rustlers!
Erg!
YUM!
Urk
SHARPENED TREE TRUNK
Uhh?
That was a close one!
Aargh!
Here, Odysseus! A bag of winds for you.
Oh, it's Aeolus, god of the winds. Thanks!
But open it carefully to release one wind at a time, won't you?

What do you reckon's in that sack?
Let's open it!
Yeah!
WHOOOOSH!
Perhaps we shouldn't have done that!
The winds blew Odysseus's ships to a land of cannibals.
Heh heh! We've eaten the crew and destroyed nearly all the ships!
Odysseus escaped and sailed to an island ruled by Circe the witch.
Where I turned most of Odysseus's crew into pigs. Tee hee!
Oink
Oink oink
Odysseus, let me help you get back your crew.
This special flower will protect you from Circe's magic.
Thanks, Hermes, messenger god!
. . . And now I want my crew turned back into men.
Oh, all right.
Oink, ooh, thank goodness!

Odysseus, before you can get home you must journey to the Underworld.
Who'd have thought that sailing from Troy to Ithaca would be this difficult?
But in the Underworld the ghosts gave him some useful tips . . .
There's trouble in Ithaca!
Make a sacrifice to Poseidon and you'll live to old age.
Whatever you do, DON'T eat the Cattle of the Sun!
Wooo!
Thanks for the advice, everyone!
Back on Circe's island . . .
I have some advice, too. Not far from here, the Sirens' song will lure you to your deaths if you hear it.
Plug your ears with beeswax! Now, farewell!
Bye, Circe, and thanks. No hard feelings about the pigs.
Tra la la
Can't hear a thing.
I wanted to hear the Sirens' song so I'm tied to the mast to stop me going to them.

Odysseus sailed on until he came to a narrow pass. On one side was Scylla.
slaver slaver
I eat sailors.
On the other side was Charybdis.
I create a perilous whirlpool.
BURP
Eek!
Urk
Bellow
Phew. We made it to the Island of the Sun.
Remember, crew, don't eat the cattle!
We've been here ages. I'm starving.
Just one little cow won't hurt . . .
YUM!
As punishment for eating the Cattle of the Sun, Zeus wrecked Odysseus's ship and drowned the crew.
I'm the only survivor.

Eventually Odysseus washed up on an island where the nymph Calypso lived.
I'm in love!
swoon swoon
Come on, Calypso. You've kept me here for seven years – please let me go home now!
I've been ordered by the gods, so I suppose I'll have to let you go.
Here, I'll help you build a raft.
Not again!
Luckily I was helped by the Phaeacians, who gave me this ship to sail home in.
Finally, Odysseus made it to Ithaca where he was welcomed by his faithful wife, Penelope, and their son, Telemachus.
And, after getting rid of Penelope's pesky suitors . . .
That was the 'trouble' the ghost warned him about . . .
We all lived happily ever after!
And making a sacrifice to Poseidon . . .

The Greeks and Romans (and everyone else)

Hello – we're the Romans.
We ended up ruling all of Greece and just about everywhere else.
The Greeks had such good stories that we carried on telling them.
And we kept their gods and goddesses too – we just gave them different names.
I'm still in charge.
ZEUS=JUPITER
And me!
HERA=JUNO
ATHENE=MINERVA
POSEIDON=NEPTUNE
Tra la la!
APOLLO=APOLLO
ARTEMIS=DIANA
Hic!
I'm still drunk.
DIONYSUS=BACCHUS
DEMETER=CERES

PERSEPHONE=PROSERPINE
ARES=MARS
HEPHAESTOS=VULCAN
I'm off to the hairdresser's.
APHRODITE=VENUS
HERMES=MERCURY
HESTIA=VESTA
Heh heh!
HADES=PLUTO

It's because of us that Neptune, Jupiter, Venus and Mars are in the solar system!
But mostly it's because of us, the Greeks!
Ha!
After the Romans, people kept on telling Greek myths.
Including me, the Great Bard, Shakespeare.

Our stories will never die.

Tracey Turner

Tracey Turner writes about lot of different subjects, including famous writers, rude words, deadly peril and, of course, the entire history of the Universe (plus some Ancient Greek monsters). She lives in Bath with Tom and their son, Toby.

Sally Kindberg

Sally Kindberg is an illustrator and writer. She once went to Elf School in Iceland, has written a book about hair, sailed on a tall ship to Lisbon and drawn the complete history of the world and the Universe. She likes getting other people to draw comic strips too, and runs workshops for them. She has a daughter called Emerald and lives in London with 91 robots.

Coming Soon . . .

the COMIC STRIP Book of Dinosaurs